A SLOANE MONROE MYSTERY

SMOKE & MIRRORS

CHERYL BRADSHAW

NEW YORK TIMES BESTSELLING AUTHOR

"LOVE IS THE CHAIN TO LOCK A
CHILD TO ITS PARENT."

—ABRAHAM LINCOLN

CHAPTER 1

Cairns, Australia

Grace Ashby was having an unusual dream. A dream so real it seemed like her mum was beside her, sleeping in the same bed she was. But her mum *wasn't* in her room. Her mum was screaming—emitting high-pitched, grisly shrieks of terror that startled Grace awake from her hellish nightmare.

The screams echoed through the hall for a few moments and then stopped, and the house returned to its usual quiet tranquility. Grace remained still, listening to the familiar creaks and groans she'd grown accustomed to over the years. Then she drifted off to sleep again, soothing her fears by assuring herself that what she had just experienced was nothing more than an all-too-realistic dream. But her self-soothing was short-lived, bursting like a popped balloon when she heard her mum shouting a slew of muffled sentences Grace couldn't string together.

Nervous about what was happening, Grace wanted to remain in bed where it was safe, where her mum had told her to stay, but something about the tone in her mum's voice wasn't right. It was different. She sounded … frightened. Grace reached a hand through the darkness until she felt the cold metal of the bedside lamp. Sliding a hand up its base, she found the switch, turned the light on, and canvassed her room.

She was alone, and the house had gone quiet again.

"Mum? Are you okay?" Grace called out. "Is something wrong?"

There was no reply.

I'm too far away from her. Maybe she can't hear me.

Grace cleared her throat, raised her voice, and repeated the question.

The outcome was the same.

Grace was afraid to leave her bed. She didn't want to walk across the long, dark corridor leading from her room to her mum's, but no matter how nervous she was, she knew sleep wouldn't find her again until she was sure her mum was all right. She peeled back the covers, took a deep breath, and crept to the door, sliding one eye out just enough for her to peer down the hall. She looked out, seeing nothing but a faint sliver of light emitting from a crack beneath her mum's door at the opposite end of the house—just enough to light the way for her.

She tiptoed down the hall, reached her mum's door, and paused, hearing the whisper of a man's voice on the opposite side. It was gruff and emotional.

Grace pressed a finger to the door, pushing it open just enough for her to glance inside. She slapped a hand across her mouth, stifling a scream as she saw her mum sprawled on the floor, unmoving. A man was hunched over her mum's body. Grace stepped into the room, and the man's head snapped back to look at her, his face grim and vexed, like her presence irritated him.

The man's name was Hugh Beaumont. Over the last two years, he and her mum had been in a relationship. Grace had liked him at first, but in recent months, his behavior had soured after he'd knelt down and proposed marriage, sliding a ring on her mum's finger before she'd had the chance to respond to his offer. Her mum had flat-out refused, taking the ring off, and handing it back to him, saying she cared for him, but she felt blindsided. She told him she wasn't ready and that he should have discussed the idea of becoming engaged with her first before making such a grandiose gesture. Undeterred, he'd grabbed her mum's hand, pushing the ring onto her palm as he said, "Keep it. Think of it as a promise ring, a sign of my commitment to our relationship."

And she'd accepted it. He'd fooled her mum, but he hadn't fooled Grace. She'd known the ring symbolized far more than a simple token of his devotion. It symbolized his power over her, a power he seemed to be exerting now.

Hugh stared at her a moment, then said, "Grace, you shouldn't be in—"

"What's wrong with my mum?" Grace asked. "What did you do to her?"

"Nothing. I didn't do anything. You don't understand."

She understood plenty. His face was sweaty and red. Her mum was unconscious, or worse. She couldn't tell yet. But there was one thing she knew for sure—*he* was to blame.

Grace charged forward. "Move! Get away from her!"

Hugh didn't budge.

"I mean it! Get out of my way, Hugh."

She stepped around him, noticing something she hadn't until now—blood—and lots of it. It had soaked through her mum's shirt, oozing drops of red onto the rug on the side of her body. Grace's knees buckled beneath her, and she collapsed to the floor. She leaned in, placing an ear over her mum's mouth. There was nothing

—no air, no signs of life. She grabbed her by the shoulders, shaking her like a rag doll. "Mum, please. Wake up. Mum!"

When there was still no response, Grace sprung to her feet, stabbing a finger into Hugh's chest. "She's not breathing! And the blood ... *you*! You did this to her!"

"Look, Grace, this isn't the time to ... I mean, I don't know how to explain ..."

He pulled a phone from his pocket and dialed a number. Before the call could go through, Grace lunged for the phone. "Give it to me! Let me have it!"

"Stop it, Grace! Stop it right now." He tipped his head toward the bedroom door. "Go back to your room and wait for me until I come get you, all right?"

He was trying to get rid of her ... *Why?*

And whom was he calling? A friend? Someone to help cover up what he just did? Was she next?

Eyes blurred with tears, Grace thrust her hands into his chest, shoving him backward. The phone clattered to the ground. She snatched it off the floor, waving it in front of him. "You're nobody! You're not my dad. You're not her husband. You're nothing, and *you* don't get to tell *me* what to do. Get out of here right now! Get out of our house!"

Hugh grabbed her arm, yanking her toward the bedroom door. She wrestled away from his grip and ran into her mum's bathroom. She slammed the door and locked it. Heartbroken and scared, Grace's thoughts turned to the only man she'd ever trusted, a man she needed more than anyone right now. Glancing around, she eyed a window on the opposite wall—a window that was just big enough for her to fit through.

CHAPTER 2

Redondo Beach, California
One week later

I stood in front of the full-sized mirror in my bedroom, staring at myself. My wedding dress was delicate and thin, with a vintage look reminiscent of a gown Grace Kelly wore in the1950s. Mine had short sleeves and was far simpler, but it was perfect, just the way I liked it. After dating Cade for the last seven years, the day we'd been talking about for so long had finally arrived. I felt ready in some ways, and not so ready in others, and even though I was happy and content, nervous jitters flowed through me like restless fireflies. In the next hour, I would wed a man I considered to be the best, most loving person I'd known in all of my life, and yet my anxiety still showed no signs of letting up anytime soon. Not only was I nervous, my OCD was in full-on mode as I fiddled with a hairpin I'd positioned and repositioned in my hair at least four times. And that was just in the last five minutes.

"Leave it alone. It's perfect," a woman's voice said.

I turned to see my closest friend standing in the doorway. Maddie was wearing a wine-colored, floor-length dress she'd chosen herself. Her long, blond hair had been curled into soft, wavy locks, a departure from her usual pigtails or braids. Yesterday she seemed a lot younger than a woman like me in her mid-forties. Today she was all grown up. We both were.

"Everything is perfect—your dress, your hair, your makeup," Maddie said as she slid up beside me at the mirror. "You don't need to change a thing."

She was right. I didn't. But we both knew I was going to do it anyway.

"Your hair is amazing," I said.

She scratched her scalp. "Well, don't get used to it. After the reception, this sophisticated princess is going back to a tracksuit and braids. I don't know how some women spend so much time on their hair every day. It took me almost two hours to pull this together, and another thirty on makeup. Other than snazzy events like this, it's a ridiculous waste of time."

I laughed. "Even Medical Examiner Barbie needs to get fixed up from time to time."

Maddie was an ME. One of the best in the country. Recently she'd ditched life in the lab and had started touring, giving lectures about her work and discussing some of the forensic breakthroughs she'd discovered over the years. She was bright and fearless. She was also a tomboy.

My grandmother entered the room and smiled. "Oh, just look at you, dear. So beautiful. You ready? It's almost time."

I nodded and repositioned the hairpin one last time.

"And where's our little man?" Gran asked.

I pointed to a chair, where Boo, my Westie, was pawing at the satin hat tied around his head, trying everything he could to get it off. I hoped it would last another thirty minutes, just long enough for us to get our rings out of it before it was destroyed.

"I may have put the hat on him too soon," I said. "He doesn't like it."

"There's no sense taking it off now," Gran said. "It's go time."

Maddie scooped Boo off the chair and looked at Gran. "I'll take him. You take her."

With no parents left in my life, and no sister, Gran would be the one walking me down the aisle.

I stood up, and my phone buzzed on the nightstand. I walked over and picked it up. The number was one I didn't recognize, and it looked international. I assumed it was probably an accidental dial and pushed it to voice mail. I looped my arm around Gran's, and she patted my hand.

"All right, then," she said. "Let's go."

We entered through the chapel doors of the old, restored church, and I scanned the room, my eyes coming to rest on a small gathering of people I loved seated in my section. They weren't family, but over the years, they'd become friends. Close friends. Even Coop—Park City's chief of police—was smiling. It was hard to believe a day had finally come where we were no longer at odds with each other. But come it had, and I couldn't have been happier.

I walked down the aisle, resting my eyes on Cade, whose smile removed the jitters inside me. He took my hand as I reached him, rubbing my palm with his fingers. The pastor began, taking us through the ceremony with ease and grace, and with Maddie's assistance, Boo walked the rings to us like he'd prepared his entire life for this moment. Not long after, we were officially a married couple, with the pastor announcing, "You may kiss the bride."

I was now Sloane Monroe-McCoy.

Cade leaned in, pausing a moment before the kiss.

"I've waited all my life to start one with you."

And as we embraced a tear trailed down my cheek because I felt the exact same way.

CHAPTER 3

Two weeks later

I returned from a relaxing but adventurous honeymoon in Africa to several missed calls on my business line from a senator in Australia named James Ashby, a man I assumed I'd never hear from again. We'd met several months earlier in Cairns when I'd traveled to Australia to help my friend, Nick Calhoun, investigate the disappearance of his wife Marissa, who was traveling Down Under to attend her friend's wedding. James was to be the groom, but once I'd solved Marissa's murder, and he'd learned his bride-to-be had been keeping secrets from him that pertained to the murder, he'd called off the wedding.

The voice mail James left me was vague: "Call me when you get this message. Something has happened here, and I'd like to hire you. I need your help."

After listening to it, I stood there, staring at my phone as if it were sand in an hourglass, while I considered whether to return the call or not. I wasn't sure I wanted to travel to another country at the moment. I also wasn't sure I wanted to offer whatever help he needed. When we'd first met, I had formed the wrong impression of him after hearing rumors about the kind of person he was, but in the end, he'd proved himself a better man than I initially believed him to be. Still, I speculated there was a side of him I hadn't seen, a side he concealed from others. I didn't know how I knew. I just did, and I wasn't sure getting involved with him again was in my best interest.

On the other hand, I'd never been one to shy away from risk. And though hard for me to admit, I'd recently come to realize my life was the most fulfilled when accompanied by a moderate amount of danger. It was something I lived for, something I needed in order to thrive, and as the sand in my imaginary hourglass began to run out, I decided I should at least talk to him before coming to a decision.

James answered the call on the second ring, saying, "Does it always take you this long to call your clients back?"

"I was on my honeymoon," I said. "I've only just returned, and you're *not* my client."

"Oh. I wasn't aware you'd gotten married. Congratulations."

"I was surprised you called. You mentioned needing my help, but you're a senator. Aren't there plenty of people who are equipped to handle your needs more than I could be?"

"There are, but none of them are you."

I accepted his flattery and got to the point. "What can I do for you?"

"You can get here as soon as possible."

"Why? What's happened?"

"A few weeks ago, my sister Caroline and the man she had been seeing were murdered in her home."

Whatever I'd expected him to say, this wasn't it.

"I … I'm really sorry to hear it," I said.

My thoughts turned to his niece, a sweet teenager with Down syndrome. I'd met her on my previous visit.

"What about Grace?" I said. "Please tell me she's all right."

"She's fine. I wouldn't say she's doing well, but we'll get there again one day. She's staying with me now, and I'm doing everything I can to help her."

"Where was Grace when Caroline was murdered?"

"She was in the house, sleeping. Caroline screamed, which woke her. She went down the hall to investigate the noise and found Caroline on the floor, bleeding and unresponsive. Hugh, Caroline's boyfriend, was crouched over her, mumbling, but Grace couldn't hear what he said."

"I thought you said he was dead."

"He is. That is to say, he was alive and appeared unharmed when Grace first discovered Caroline, but he's dead now."

"I'm confused," I said.

"I was too. There are a lot of moving pieces here. A lot of things which don't make sense, but they will once we find the man who did this."

Or woman.

"How are you sure it was a man?" I asked.

"I'm not. It's just a hunch."

"What else can you tell me?"

"From what Grace has been able to piece together, we know Hugh was alive initially. When Grace saw him leaning over Caroline, she assumed Hugh had killed her. She locked herself in the bathroom and escaped through the window. She ran to a neighbor's house and called me. I headed straight over. When I arrived, Hugh was dead. He'd been found at the bottom of the stairs, and it looks like he either fell down them or was pushed."

I visualized Hugh having a confrontation with Caroline's killer. I assumed a chase had ensued at some point, wherein Hugh ended at the bottom of the stairs.

"Grace never heard or saw anyone else in the house?" I asked.

"No one. But her memory of the night's events hasn't been great. She was quite shaken up. It's still a bit fuzzy."

"It's understandable. I'm sure she's confused about everything right now."

I found the whole thing strange. Caroline had been dead when Grace found her, but Hugh had been alive. Minutes later, he was also dead, but the two had died in different ways. I wondered if Grace was confused at the time, so overcome with shock and grief at seeing her mother dead on the floor that she'd missed things. Clues. Maybe the killer had still been there in the house before she escaped out the window. I also wondered if Hugh had been an intended victim, or if he'd been killed because he was in the wrong place at the wrong time. Or maybe he hadn't been murdered at all. Maybe he'd just suffered a heart attack or something and just toppled.

"I'm sorry your family is grieving," I said, "but I'm not sure what I can do to help. I'm not a licensed private investigator in your country."

"It doesn't matter. You don't need to worry about that."

Too late—I already was, and the last thing I wanted to do was to end up on the wrong side of the law in a country where I wasn't a citizen.

"Is there a way I can help you from here in the States?" I asked.

"No. You must come to Cairns. It makes the most sense. You didn't seem to have a problem working in Australia before, hmm?"

He was right. I didn't, and I justified my actions because I was helping Nick find answers about what happened to his wife. That was personal. This wasn't.

"I'm not sure, Senator Ashby. It's not that I don't want to help. I do. I just don't know if it's a good idea for me to—"

"Look, Sloane, all I want you to do is to do some digging around. I thought I knew almost everything there was to know about my sister, and now I believe I was mistaken. I don't know who did this to her, or why, or if it has anything to do with me, or if it doesn't. The police have been remarkable. They're doing everything they can. But I'm impatient, and I want the killer found—now. The longer this goes unsolved, the less the chances are that we'll find out who did this. I need you. Will you come?"

Guilt often caused people to break from the norm, shredding their ethical rulebook and creating one more suited to the situation, like he was doing now. And even though I was principled and tried to do the right thing in most situations, it was something we had in common. His comment about whether Caroline's murder had anything to do with him meant the idea was weighing on him. I was familiar with that particular kind of weight, what it felt like, and how far it had dragged me down when my sister died at the hands of a serial killer several years before. Until he had answers, the weight he felt would eat away at him like rust on a sunken ship, and I didn't want to add to that.

"Let me see what I can do," I said. "I'll get back to you as soon as I can."

CHAPTER 4

Two days later, I touched down at the airport in Cairns. An older man in his late sixties wearing a weathered bush hat and a bright, tropical, button-up shirt—only the bottom four buttons were fastened, so his white chest hair poked through the top—was waiting next to the luggage carousel. He looked like a senior-aged model for Tommy Bahama. He introduced himself as Froggy and said he would take me to meet with Senator Ashby, but I had somewhere else in mind I wanted to go first.

On the way to the car, I made my intentions clear, which didn't seem to please him.

"James has been waiting for you to arrive," he said. "It's best not to keep him waiting, all right."

"I just want to make a quick pit stop. It won't take long, and I feel the senator would appreciate me getting right to work."

He frowned, so I presented him with another option. "If you don't want to drive me, I can grab a cab or an Uber and meet up with the senator once I've finished."

Froggy sent a quick text message, which I assumed went to the senator. He received a reply moments later and said he'd drive me where I wanted to go, then afterward would take me to see the senator.

Twenty minutes later, a freckled, redheaded Victoria Bennett glanced up at me from her desk, giving me a look that made me feel like I was expected. Victoria was the coroner for the North Queensland region, and although we hadn't spent much time together on my last visit, she was a straight shooter, and I hoped she'd be willing to fill me in on what she knew so far.

"Nice to see you again so soon, Sloane," she said.

"You too," I said. "Your hair is different."

She blushed. I assumed it was because the last time I was there, she was sporting a *Pulp Fiction* type bob. Now her hair was as short as mine and styled much the same.

She brushed her bangs to the side with her hand and said, "I hope you don't mind. It's just … when I saw your pixie cut the last time you were here, I finally got up the nerve to chop my own hair. I've been wanting to do it for years."

"Of course I don't mind. It looks great on you."

And it did.

She was even more stunning than I remembered.

"James told me you were stopping by," she admitted. "News travels fast in this place."

"Did he tell you why I'm here?"

"Not at first, but I know what you do. It wasn't hard to figure out. When I asked him, he didn't say much, but he didn't deny it, either."

"I was hoping we could talk about what you've learned about Caroline's and Hugh's deaths."

She stared at me for a moment but didn't respond, and then her gaze shifted to something behind me. I glanced over my shoulder and saw Froggy hovering by the door. We made eye contact, and he started whistling, like piping out a tune was going to make his eavesdropping just fine and dandy. It wasn't fine … or dandy, and I wondered if he was really a driver or someone the senator had sent to shadow me during my visit, as his casual attire suggested. If so, he'd soon learn I didn't work that way.

"Can I help you?" I asked. "This is a personal conversation."

"Oh," Froggy said. "I … uhh … just wanted to know how long you think you'll be here."

I shrugged. "I can't say. As long as it takes. I'm aware the senator wants to meet with me today, and I will, just as soon as I finish talking with Victoria."

"It's just … you're expected, and you shouldn't keep him waiting for too long."

"I'm jetlagged, sweaty, and in dire need of a shower, but I'm here, already working, doing the job he hired me to do. He should be happy about that."

"He is. It's just … he shifted his schedule around today to accommodate your arrival."

"He never told me he'd moved his appointments," I said.

"He wouldn't. He's too modest. I'm not."

Obviously.

"For a driver, you seem to care a lot about the senator."

He tipped his head back and let out a full-bellied laughed. Victoria followed suit, letting me know I was missing something they both knew and I didn't.

"What's so funny?" I asked.

"I'm not James' driver. I'm his father."

I was starting to feel like I'd been right before in thinking that James had sent someone he trusted to keep an eye on me. Perhaps it was to protect me while I did my investigating. Or perhaps his reasons were entirely different.

"You could have told me who you were earlier," I said.

He shrugged. "I could tell you a lot of things. Doesn't mean I will."

"You can go."

"I'm sorry. What?"

"You can go. I have the senator's address. When I'm ready to see him, I'll give him a call."

"I was just teasing you a little. You know that, right?"

Victoria seemed to sense the tension between us. She walked over and stood next to me. "Sloane, you're probably hungry after such a long flight."

I had been flown in first-class and had taken full advantage of the upgrade, but she was offering me a way out of an uncomfortable situation, and I knew better than not to take it. "I'm starving."

"Great." She turned toward Froggy. "I'm taking her to lunch, Noel, and then I'll drop her off to see James."

Noel—we had a name. A real name.

He grimaced, yanked his phone out of the pocket of his cargo shorts, and sent another text. Seconds later, my phone rang. I didn't answer it. I didn't need to. I knew who was calling.

"Aren't you going to get that?" Noel asked.

I shook my head. "I don't like being followed around and spied upon. I'm not at your son's beck and call just because I'm working a case for him. I'm sure that's what he expects, but that doesn't work for me."

Noel crossed his arms in front of him. "Understood. Just so you know, I wasn't *spying*. I was just trying to give you a lift after your long flight."

He walked out of Victoria's office without saying another word. She grabbed her wallet and car keys and said, "Well, that was fun."

CHAPTER 5

Victoria and I ordered a couple of lattes at a café in the city, and then we strolled along a wooden walking path next to the pier. We sipped our drinks and soaked up the tropical sun. I thought about how far away I felt from home and how different things were here than the hustle and bustle in the States. In Cairns life seemed to almost come to a standstill at times. The air seemed different because it was. A place like this gave one time to think—really think. To put things into perspective. I thought about the last time I'd been here, and of Marissa, and how she had probably walked the same path I was walking now on the night she had been murdered.

How fleeting life was, and how fragile. One day we're alive and free, the next we're turned to dust, evaporating into an afterlife I wasn't even sure existed. Some days I felt larger than life, like I meant something and like I mattered. Today I felt small and insignificant, like I could exit life's door tomorrow, and in a hundred years, there would be little left of me to remind anyone of my existence. Thinking about it now, I vowed to make my mark in some small way. I wanted to *be* better—to make a difference—not just for myself, but for all those around me.

I glanced at Victoria who was eyeing me curiously, like she could tell my mind had drifted and she was wondering how far.

"I was surprised James asked you to come here," Victoria said.

"Why?" I asked.

"I don't know. He doesn't let many people in—not when it comes to his personal life, and the murder of his sister ... well, I can't think of anything more personal than that."

"It doesn't feel like he's letting me in. It feels like I'm just one more card in the deck he's been dealt recently, and after some thought, he's decided to play multiple hands to see which one gives him the best results in the fastest time frame."

"You think so?"

"I do. He wants to know what happened, and he wants to know *now*. The police are doing everything they can, I'm sure, but he's impatient. He wants another perspective. That's where I come in. How's it been since everything happened?"

"It has been a trying couple of weeks for all of us. He's not the only one pushing for answers. Everyone is. It's a tremendous amount of pressure."

"I'm sure he feels like he's in a fishbowl right now," I said. "Cairns may be a city, but it's also a small, close-knit community. There was a table of women in the coffee shop discussing the details of the murder while we waited for our lattes, and when we walked outside, a man was showing his wife the front page of the local paper. Have you seen it?"

She nodded. "I haven't read the latest article, but I've seen the photos they posted of Caroline and Hugh. You don't miss a lot, do you?"

"I wouldn't be any good at my job if I did. Everywhere I look, people are talking about what happened. They're all speculating and drawing their own conclusions. It's almost like what happened to

Caroline has also happened to them. Whether they knew her or didn't, it's still personal to them."

"That's an interesting way of looking at it."

It was also an accurate one, and it made Cairns special, different than most other places where I'd been involved in an investigation.

"You called the senator by his first name a few times today," I said. "Aside from your forensic work on the case, are you two friends?"

She bit her upper lip.

They *were* connected somehow.

She stared at her latte. "I feel like I need a much stronger drink if I'm going to talk about it."

"Is it that bad?" I asked.

"It's not bad. Not really. I ... uhh ... we dated for a while. Well, not a long while. A couple of months a few years ago."

"What ..."

Happened.

I left the word I didn't say alone. What *happened* wasn't my business. If she wanted to tell me, she could. And though I was curious, I wasn't going to pry. Not with her love life, anyway.

"It's all right," she said. "I don't mind talking to you about it. We met at a holiday fund-raiser for the city after he became senator. He was single, and I was going through a divorce at the time, and I wasn't in the right place in my life to start a new relationship. He was, and after dating for a short time, he wanted a commitment. I wasn't ready. I couldn't give him what he wanted, so I broke things off, even though I can admit now that I really didn't want to."

Years had passed, but from the look on her face, the pain of her decision to end the relationship was still fresh in her mind, even now.

"Must have been hard," I said. "I've been there before."

"I still wonder if I should have done things differently. We weren't together long, but the bond we shared together was unlike anything I've experienced before or since."

"Have you ever thought about talking to him or trying to get back what you once had?"

"I almost called him a few times, but I didn't."

"What stopped you?" I asked.

"I have no interest being in the public eye the way he is in his career right now. If he were no longer senator, maybe it would be different." She paused, then abruptly switched subjects. "Hey, you want to sit down for a few minutes?"

I nodded, and we crossed into a park-like picnic area along the esplanade. I spotted a vacant table nestled under a ficus tree, and we sat down.

"What can you tell me about Caroline's death?"

"She was knifed in the chest."

"How many times?"

"Once."

"She died from a single stab wound?" I asked.

"She did. The knife punctured her abdominal aorta, which means she would have died shortly thereafter. Looking at how specific Caroline's injury was, I would assume the killer knew where the knife needed to enter her body in order to be fatal. The puncture wound was clean. With Hugh, it was different."

"Was the knife recovered from the crime scene?"

"It was found outside, in Caroline's back garden. The length and width of the blade are consistent with the wounds found on Caroline, but there were no prints on the knife's handle. Not even a smudge."

"So, someone took the time to wipe their prints off the blade but was careless enough to leave it behind?"

Victoria lifted a finger. "I'll get to my theory on that in a minute. Another interesting thing of note is that Caroline had no defensive wounds, but Hugh had a slice on his neck that wasn't deep, like he had been trying to fight his attacker off before he tumbled down the stairs to his death."

"How many cuts did he have?"

"Only one, and like I said, it wasn't deep. It was more like a scrape than a stab wound. Hugh is a lot bigger than Caroline, and if he did have the chance to fight for his life, the killer would have had a harder time doing what he'd come to do."

"Hugh died from falling down the stairs, right?"

She nodded. "His neck was broken. From what Grace told us, we know Hugh was still alive when she discovered her mum. And yet, at some point after Grace climbed out of the bathroom window, Hugh was also murdered."

"I suppose it's possible the killer was in the house the entire time, hiding out somewhere," I said.

If true, the question was—*why?*

And had the killer intended to kill Grace as well?

"This leads to my theory about why the knife was left behind," she said. "I believe the police arrived shortly after Hugh was killed. The killer was still in the house, and he panicked. He escaped, wiping the handle of the knife off as he ran out the back door. He dropped the knife, which I believe was an accident. At some point, he would have realized his mistake, but with cops swarming the place, it was too late to go back for it."

There was a glaring, obvious question we hadn't addressed yet. Why had Grace's life been spared? Maybe the killer had intended on killing them all, but when Grace escaped through the bathroom window, he lost the opportunity.

"What do you know about Caroline and Hugh's whereabouts on the night they died?" I asked.

"We know Caroline took Grace to a movie around seven. It got over at half past nine, which put them home around ten. Adelaide Wiggins, one of Caroline's neighbors, corroborated this."

"Was Adelaide's house where Grace ran to after climbing out the bathroom window?"

Victoria nodded. "Adelaide was in the kitchen, ending a call with her daughter, when Caroline and Grace returned home from the movie. She checked the time of the call and said they would have arrived home a few minutes before ten. She said she watched Caroline and Grace get out of the car and go into the house. She saw no one else, and nothing seemed out of the ordinary."

"What do you know about what followed?"

"Grace told the police she had fallen asleep in the car on the way back from the movie, and she went to bed as soon as they got home. Not long after, she woke to the sound of her mother screaming."

"What time did Grace call the senator?"

"Half past eleven."

"So both murders took place within an hour or so of Caroline arriving home."

"Right, and it fits with the overall condition of the bodies when I found them. Both were showing early signs of lividity, particularly Caroline, but there were no signs of rigor mortis yet."

"When did Hugh arrive at the house?"

"He was on a flight back home from Sydney when Caroline and Grace would have returned after the movie. The plane arrived in Cairns a few minutes after ten. He had no checked bags, and there's video surveillance showing him getting into his car at a quarter past ten. Police believe he went straight from the airport to Caroline's house. Hugh had a key, so it's likely he let himself in. What we don't know is whether Caroline was alive when he arrived—if she'd been attacked yet or if she was already dead."

This led to another possibility. If Hugh had arrived and Caroline was dying or dead, and the killer was still there, perhaps Caroline had been the only intended victim, and Hugh had suffered the same fate because the killer was still in the house when he arrived and hadn't made his escape yet.

Or maybe Hugh had killed Caroline and was so distraught at what he'd done that he threw himself down the stairs.

"Grace is sure she didn't see or hear anyone else in the house?" I asked.

"She swears the only person she saw was Hugh."

"She heard her mom scream. How long was it before she went to check on her and discovered she was dead?"

"That part we're a bit unsure about. At first, Grace didn't know whether she was dreaming or if what she'd heard was real. When she realized something might have been wrong, initially she was scared. She didn't go to her mum's room right away, and we aren't sure how many minutes passed before she was brave enough to walk down the hall and check things out."

"Where are the police in the way of suspects?"

"Not far. As far as they can tell from those they've interviewed, everyone loved Caroline. They're struggling to even find a motive for her death. Hugh, on the other hand, didn't have the best reputation around him. Some people liked him, others didn't. He was known to have an aggressive side in his younger years."

"Aggressive how?" I asked.

"I went to school with Hugh. He was the kindest person one minute, and the next, he'd explode over something insignificant."

Sounded perfectly bipolar to me.

"He dated one of my friends back then," she said. "At one point, he even proposed, and for about a month, they were engaged."

"What happened?"

"She didn't say much about the breakup. She just said he was controlling and called all the shots in the relationship. That was twenty years ago, though. People change."

Sometimes. Other times they don't.

"Do you have any idea how he treated Caroline?" I asked.

"I saw them out in the city a few times when they first got

together. From what I could tell when I saw them, they seemed to have a good thing going."

"Have you heard of any incidents involving Hugh since high school?"

"Only one. Last year, police were called to a brewery downtown. Caroline had walked up to the bar to get a round of drinks, and a guy put his hand on Caroline's shoulder. Assuming the guy was hitting on her, Hugh came over and threw a punch at the guy without even saying a word. Both men were tossed out of the bar, and when the police arrived, Hugh was arrested, but the guy he punched dropped the charges. I guess he was also a therapist. Hugh apologized, and the guy let it go."

In the time we'd been sitting together, Victoria had continually rubbed her hands together, one over the other, like a nervous tic. She'd told me far more than I had expected, but I believed something big was missing from the overall narrative. What I couldn't figure out was whether it was something she couldn't tell me, didn't want to tell me, or just couldn't bring herself to say. I didn't have her trust yet, and she didn't have mine, but a level of comfort existed between us that had formed the first time we'd met. I decided it was best not to try and get it out of her just yet, figuring I had a better chance of her revealing whatever it was in her own time.

"I appreciate you sharing information with me," I said. "You didn't have to, and it really helps me out that you did. It gives me a good place to start."

"James must think a lot of you. He wouldn't have asked you to come all this way otherwise."

I wasn't sure what he thought of me, but he'd seen how committed I was at working my cases all the way through.

"Speaking of him, I should probably get moving. Is there anything else I should know before we go?"

We sat in silence for a time while she pondered the question. Ordinarily, I found silence between two people for any length of time to be awkward, but as awkward as it was, I thought waiting it out might be just what she needed to say what hadn't been said. Sadly, I was disappointed.

"I think that's all for now," she said. "If there's anything else, I have your number."

We returned to the car and drove out of the parking garage. One minute, we were engaging in small talk as she wound around the streets of the city, and the next, I was drifting in and out of consciousness. The car came to a stop, and when my eyes opened, I glanced around, realizing she hadn't taken me to James' office. She'd driven me to my hotel.

"I thought you were taking me to meet James," I said.

"I was, but you're exhausted, Sloane. You might want to get some rest first and see James later. I can let him know I talked to you and dropped you at the hotel, if you like."

I shook my head. At this point, it was better coming from me. "That's okay. I'll go check in, splash some water on my face, and see if he still wants to see me today. Maybe we can talk over the phone and visit in person tomorrow."

I grabbed my bag and stepped out of the car. As I turned to walk toward the hotel, Victoria's passenger-side window came down. She leaned over and said, "Hey, Sloane, there's umm … one more thing, something that's been bugging me that you should probably know."

I assumed I was about to find out what she hadn't told me earlier. "What is it?"

"It's Caroline's autopsy. She wasn't just stabbed."

"What do you mean?"

"There was a considerable amount of bruising on her back and chest, and a bruise on one of her shoulders in the shape of a thumbprint."

"Do you think they were related to the night of the murder?"

"I don't. They weren't fresh, meaning they weren't inflicted the night she was killed. I believe Caroline was in some kind of physical altercation recently."

I assumed the senator knew of the bruising, but he hadn't mentioned it over the phone. "Any idea how old the bruises are?"

"Fresh bruises tend to be reddish-blue or purple in color. The bruises on Caroline were brownish-green. Bruises can be tricky things to put a timeline on, but based on the discoloration of her skin, I'd guess they were at least a week old. I don't know if what happened prior to her death has anything to do with why she was murdered, but something happened to Caroline *before* the night she died, and no one seems to know anything about it."

CHAPTER 6

I tipped my head back on the pillow, thinking I would relax for a few minutes before calling the senator, but it didn't take long before I succumbed to the sleep I so desperately needed. I woke sometime later to a dark room and the sound of someone knocking on my hotel room door. I stumbled out of bed and switched on a floor lamp, glancing in the mirror as I willed my unrested body toward the door. From the looks of things, I'd seen better days. A lot better. I had black mascara smeared across one of my cheeks, and my short, dark hair looked like it had been sucked into a vacuum. It wasn't ideal or presentable, but there wasn't time to do anything about it.

I opened the door, and the senator looked me up and down, blinking a few times like he was unsure how to react to the hot mess standing before him.

He narrowed his eyes and said, "Were you *sleeping*?"

His tone of voice made me feel like a schoolgirl being scolded by the principal.

"I meant to meet up with you earlier," I said. "I really did."

"And then?"

"I sat on the bed and fell asleep."

He shook his head. "I'm confused."

"About what?"

"Were you planning to meet with me right after you went to see Victoria, or after the two of you took a leisurely stroll in the park, or after you dropped by your hotel for some shut-eye? Or not at all? If you needed sleep, all you had to do was tell me, but you should have checked in and let me know what was going on, at the very least."

He looked irritated.

I didn't blame him.

He also seemed a lot skinnier than I remembered, or maybe the difference was the muscle tone he used to have now appeared to be gone. Losing a loved one changed a person, and generally, it wasn't for the better.

"I should have met with you right after I arrived," I said. "I just thought I'd get right to work, so I went to see Victoria, and I lost track of time. Then she dropped me off here, and I—"

"My idea of you getting 'right to work' would have been for you to meet with me shortly after you landed."

Lack of sleep often went hand in hand with a lack of me being able to keep my mouth shut when it was better to do so. I felt myself reeling, and there was little I could do to stop it. Even so, it was worth a try. "I was going to call you when I arrived at the hotel, and like I said, I fell asleep. I didn't mean to ... it just happened."

"You're *working* for me. I expect better communication than this."

Rebuked a second time.

My attempt at self-control had all but dissolved.

"You hired me, yes," I said, "but I *work* for myself, and I'll do things the way I see fit. And by the way, I don't need your father following me around, keeping tabs on what I'm doing. I can't do my job if I feel like I'm being scrutinized and tattled on."

"You honestly think I sent my dad to pick you up at the airport so he could keep an eye on you?" He bowed his head and sighed. "Since Caroline died, my dad's been worried—about me, about Grace, about everyone and everything. When he's not with Grace, he's hanging around my office. And while I appreciate his concern, I'm not getting enough work done. I thought having him pick you up would give him something to do while offering you transportation at the same time. It was an attempt to be polite and make sure you had someone to help you get where you needed to go."

He had a superb ability for making me feel small. If there were a hole, I would have crawled into it. All I could do now was to try to make peace.

"I'm sorry. I didn't know."

"Dad's a retired chief superintendent of police. Having him with you today kept you safe."

"Why didn't you tell me any of this before I arrived, or even when I arrived?"

"I didn't realize I needed to in order for you not to make false assumptions."

Nothing I said seemed to make things better.

"I shouldn't have brought you here," he said. "I think it would be best if you went home."

He turned and started to walk away, leaving me there, speechless, and feeling like a real idiot.

The man was grieving, and while I hadn't slept for hours, he looked like he hadn't slept in days.

I stepped into the hallway and called after him. "Wait, Senator Ashby. Please. I'm sorry. I shouldn't have kept you waiting today, and I want you to know I'm fully committed to helping you in any way I can. Give me another chance to prove it to you."

He didn't look back. He didn't even acknowledge me. He rounded the corner and disappeared. I did the walk of shame back into my hotel room and closed the door, disappointed with my behavior. I sat on the bed, pondering whether there was anything I could do to salvage what had just happened. Around my third or fourth bad idea, there was a knock on my door again.

CHAPTER 7

How's Grace?" I asked.

The senator sat on a chair, considering my question. "All right, I suppose. She's emotional. Missing her mother. She knows what happened, but she's confused about it. When she thinks back to that night, she says it all feels like a dream. She wakes up sometimes in the middle of the night and calls out for Caroline. Sleep makes her forget Caroline isn't around anymore."

"I can't imagine how hard it must be for her to make sense of it all," I said.

"In some ways, I suppose I'm in denial too. Even after the funeral, and even though I *know* my sister's gone, I'm struggling to accept it. I guess it's because I don't want it to be true. I want to look up from my desk and see her sweet smile and hear her voice as she tells me she's stopped by my office to bring me a coffee or to take me to lunch."

I had experienced the same pain he was feeling now, so I knew what he was going through. I also knew he was bound to feel worse before he felt better. My thoughts turned to Grace.

"Will you be keeping your niece, or will she be going to live with someone else in the family?" I asked.

"I have an older sister and a younger brother who have both offered to take her, but I'm keeping Grace with me. I'm closer to her than they are. It's better this way, especially since she has Down syndrome. I understand what she needs better than they do."

He turned, staring out the window at nothing, and for a moment, we sat in silence, listening to the sound of bats shrieking in the distance.

A couple minutes went by before he spoke again.

"Grace keeps asking to go to the house," he said.

"Why?"

"She says it's to get more of her things, but I believe it's because the house reminds her of Caroline, and because it's home. The only home she's ever known."

"Why haven't you taken her?"

"In my opinion, it would have a negative effect on her. It's not my intention to deny her what she needs, but right now, my focus is on helping her get her life back to whatever kind of normal it can be, even though I expect it to be a process, one that takes some time."

"Is there anything I can do for her while I'm here?"

"You can help solve her mother's murder so we can put all this behind us and move on."

When he spoke of the murders, his focus was solely on Caroline. It was almost as if Hugh hadn't died along with her. I understood why his sister was his primary concern, but it seemed odd how dismissive he was about Hugh. It was possible they hadn't had a good relationship. Or maybe I was making something out of nothing, and James hadn't said much about him because he knew once we found the killer, both murders would be solved.

"What was your relationship with Hugh?" I asked.

He stared at me like I had asked a trick question. "Why do you ask?"

"I still don't know much about him."

"There's not much to say. We weren't close. I didn't know him well. I never thought Hugh was a good fit for my sister. Caroline was well aware of my feelings, but she didn't agree, and after I voiced my concerns about their relationship, she made it clear she wasn't interested in hearing what I thought of him. After that, he wasn't a topic we discussed."

"What didn't you like about him?"

"My disdain wasn't about one specific thing as much as it was about how different they were as people. Hugh was a laborer. He worked in construction. Caroline was a psychologist. One of the best in the country."

"Are you saying you had a problem with him because he wasn't in the same working class?"

He nodded. "People say opposites attract, and who knows, maybe they do in some situations. I just didn't see her with him long-term. He didn't fit into our world."

I wondered what world he thought I fit into and whether he considered me to be on a much lower level than himself.

"Did Hugh know how you felt about him?"

"I'm sure he did. I've never been one to hide the way I feel. I don't see the point. The last time I saw him was at a barbecue for Grace's birthday. I spoke to him just like I'd speak to anyone else. Even though I wasn't fond of him, I was always polite whenever the two of us were together."

I switched topics. "I know Grace is going through a difficult time, but I'd like to talk to her. I'd be careful to keep things simple. What do you think?"

He leaned forward, resting his hands on his knees. "Grace is too fragile right now, Sloane. I'll help you in any way I can, but she has been through enough in recent weeks. I don't want her answering any more questions about what happened that night. Not unless she absolutely has to do it."

It was the response I expected, and I understood his desire to protect her. But in order to get the full story, I needed to hear the details of that night from her perspective, instead of hearing it second-hand through everyone else. For now, I would have to wait.

"Did you know Victoria found bruises on Caroline's body during the autopsy?"

"I did."

"Any idea where they came from?"

He crossed one leg over the other and sighed, which seemed to answer my question. He didn't know, and it bothered him.

"She didn't say anything to me about the bruises," he said. "I wasn't made aware until Victoria showed them to me."

"Victoria said one of the bruises looks like it's in the shape of a thumbprint. If that's true, it would lead me to suspect Caroline had an altercation with someone before she died."

"Speculating it's a thumbprint and proving it are two different things. Victoria hasn't been able to prove it yet."

"Let's say it is. Could Hugh have done it?"

"I would like to think if he had, she would have told me."

I disagreed. Caroline knew her brother didn't like Hugh. If Hugh was capable of inflicting the bruises, there's a chance she would have kept it secret, out of fear of what would happen if she revealed it, or out of not wanting to disappoint her brother even further than she already had. She may have even been ashamed.

"What was their relationship like right before she died?"

"Grace told me Caroline planned on ending things with Hugh."

"Did Grace know when Caroline was going to do it?" I asked.

"The night Caroline was murdered, she planned on asking Hugh to give back the house key and ending the relationship as soon as he arrived. She knew Hugh had a temper and wasn't sure how he'd take the news, so she told Grace if she overheard them arguing not to worry and to just stay in bed."

But Caroline had *screamed*, which made Grace too worried to stay in bed.

He stuck a hand inside his pocket, pulled out a set of keys, and set them on the table next to me. "The yellow-ringed key is to my sister's house at 111 Providence Road. The blue key will get you into the room in the office she works at on the corner of Lake and Sheridan. Detectives have been through both places and have removed anything they felt was relevant to the case, but I'd like you to poke around to see if there's anything of interest they may have missed."

"Have *you* gone through her house and her office already?"

He nodded. "I didn't see anything of note. But I've been to both places many times in the past. Maybe it's too familiar to me. You might be drawn to something I wouldn't notice. When you came here before, searching for the murderer of your friend's wife, you put things together in a way no one else did. I'm hoping you'll do the same for me."

I hoped so too.

"I'd also like to ask you for a favor," he said.

"What is it?"

"I stopped by the house and brought over some of Grace's clothes a couple of weeks ago, but a lot of her personal items are still in the house. Would you pack up what's left inside her closet and bring it over? I'd ask my dad, but he hasn't gone to Caroline's place since she was murdered, and I'm not sure he can handle being there yet. I'd do it myself, but I figure since you're going to be there … well, it would really help me out."

"It's no problem, Senator Ashby. I'd be happy to help."

"One more thing. Call me James, all right?"

I nodded.

He glanced at his watch, a Rolex, with a silver and gold band and a shiny blue dial that looked like it was about ten times out of my price range.

"I have to go." He stood and walked to the door. "I'm heading home. Dad's with Grace now, but she'll be wondering why I'm not there yet. She's easily worried these days. What happened to Caroline has her worried it could happen to any of us next. It doesn't matter what I say or how much I comfort her. She doesn't feel safe."

CHAPTER 8

The man pressed his binoculars against the glass and stared through them, watching the dark-haired woman in the hotel room across the street say something to Senator James Ashby before they said their goodbyes. If only he could have listened in on their conversation. Then maybe he'd have answers to some of his burning questions.

The man had been following the dark-haired woman since midday, from the time she'd arrived at the coroner's office, a building he'd been monitoring here and there to see who'd come and gone after the murders took place. So far he'd learned little about the woman he'd been following other than one distinct detail: her nasal accent was annoying. She was Canadian or American, he guessed. Either way, she was a foreigner, and he'd never cared much for foreigners.

Earlier in the day when the man pretended to stretch his legs against a tree in the park, he'd caught bits and pieces of the foreigner's conversation with Victoria Bennett. The foreigner had been asking questions—*too many questions* to pass for idol curiosity, and Victoria's mouth ran like a faucet, giving the foreigner private information, things not yet revealed to the public.

Questions littered the man's mind.

Why was the foreigner in Cairns?

Why was she asking so many questions?

Why had she visited the coroner?

And what had she been doing with Senator Ashby in her hotel room?

The man made a few minor tweaks and adjustments to the binoculars and then brought it back up to his eyes again. The foreigner had moved closer to the window, giving him a more candid look at her. She was a little taller than the average woman and slender, but not *too* slender. He could tell from the shirt she wore that she had noticeable curves, and a rather large bum, considering how slender she was. He guessed her age to be somewhere around forty, or a bit older, even. She was an appealing woman, despite sporting a sassy, short haircut, but he'd seen prettier in his own country. Since he found her hairstyle to be off-putting, he'd subtracted a few points from her overall score.

The man didn't understand the fascination for women to work so hard to be so different nowadays. Short hair. Shaved, punk-rock styles. Hair dyed every color in the rainbow. It was artificial and unattractive. Gone were the days of natural beauties like Grace Kelly. Now *there* was a princess who knew how to behave.

The foreigner had been leaning against the chair in her hotel room for a few minutes now. Maybe she was just tired. She certainly *looked* tired, and like a dog that needed to be groomed. Another minute passed, and she crossed the room, pausing to look at the alarm clock on her nightstand, before reaching down and turning it so that it faced forward, fully aligned with the lamp adjacent to it.

She's a perfectionist. Interesting.

Now here was a characteristic trait the man could get behind.

He was a bit obsessive-compulsive himself.

The foreigner walked to the window and drew the curtains closed, shutting the man out for the night and leaving him to ponder what to do if the suspicions he had about her proved to be correct. If he was right—and to his credit he usually was—getting rid of her seemed like an easy option and a simple solution to the problem. If he did go that route, it would have to be later. At the moment something far more important impregnated his mind, something he'd put off for too long.

A steadfast follower of boundaries and rules, the man always believed in giving credit where credit was due. But giving credit where it *wasn't* due? Well, that just seemed wrong, and the time had come for him to make it right.

The man walked to the small, flimsy desk in the corner of the living room and sat down, pulling a pad of paper and pen out of the drawer. He clicked the pen and was just about to jot down the perfect message when he noticed the hotel's name embossed at the center of the bottom of the page. He flipped through the rest of the tablet. Every page was the exact same, and that simply would not do. Riffling through the other drawers in the room, he came across a phone directory and opened it. The contents page at the beginning had just enough room on the right-hand side to suit his needs if he wrote small enough. With care, he tore the page out and began writing, pausing a moment when he felt a presence behind him.

He glanced over his shoulder and said, "Oh, Petey. It's you. I'm busy right now. We'll talk later. Run along."

Petey acknowledged the man with a nod and disappeared into the bedroom. The man felt a small amount of remorse for blowing Petey off like he had, but he didn't want anyone spoiling his plans. Not when they were about to get so exciting.

CHAPTER 9

The next morning I stepped out of the shower, pressed a towel to my wet hair, and hurried to the nightstand, trying to answer the call before it went to voice mail.

Out of breath, I managed to utter a simple, "Good morning, Senator."

"James," he corrected.

"*James*. Right."

"How are you today?" he asked. "Feeling more rested than yesterday?"

"Much better today."

"I received an unexpected call this morning from the police. There's been a development in my sister's case."

"What kind of development?"

"It seems the killer may have reached out."

"What do you mean? What's happened?"

"This morning, the local paper received a handwritten note on a page that had been torn out of a telephone book."

"What did it say?" I asked.

"'A fool doth think he is wise, but the wise man knows himself to be a fool.'"

The quote was a familiar one.

"He's quoting Shakespeare," I said.

"So I've been told. What do you make of it?"

I ran the lines of the quote in my head a few times.

"My interpretation is that the wise man knows he still has a lot to learn, but the foolish man is hard-headed. He thinks he knows everything already and isn't open to learning something new."

"What do you think he means by that?"

I wasn't sure.

"Was anything else written along with it?" I asked. "Did he include a signature?"

"Those were the only words written on the page."

"Then why is the paper assuming it's related to the killer?"

"The note was shoved into the crack of the door at the newspaper agency. Folded up along with it was a photo of Caroline and Hugh that the newspaper had published a day before."

I'd read everything the paper had reported on during the flight overseas, which wasn't much. It was more speculation than hard facts. They'd reported on the double homicide, the knife found at the scene, the neighbor who was with Grace when she called the police, and a bit of background information on Caroline and Hugh—the type of people they were and a few details of their life.

Assuming the mysterious note was from the man I was tracking, something the newspaper had reported on was either wrong or was a detail the killer didn't like, and it had bothered him enough that he was compelled to have it corrected. The fact he'd reached out was good, and I hoped it would continue.

"Has anything been reported inaccurately to the paper that you know of?" I asked. "Or has anything been said on purpose to draw him out?"

"The paper has omitted a few details, at the request of police."

His response was vague. It didn't answer the question I'd asked. I tried again.

"But has the paper lied or misrepresented anything about the case? The killer took the time to write a note and deliver it, which means he's willing to take a risk. It also means he cares about the media attention he's receiving. I believe he wants to take credit for what he's done, but not for what he hasn't."

He paused, then said, "There may have been one small thing. It wasn't my doing. The chief superintendent made the decision. The latest news article said a neighbor might have seen the killer fleeing the crime. It isn't true. It never happened."

"Why would the police want to fabricate that?"

"To mess with the killer, to get him to do what he's doing right now, reaching out. I wasn't sure it was a great idea at first. But it worked."

The killer's ego had prompted him to reach out—he cared about which information was fact and which was fiction. It was the start of a profile I could build on. Now all I needed to do was fill in the gaps.

CHAPTER 10

No matter how many crime scenes I had witnessed in my career, seeing them had never become easier. Standing at the very place a person took their last breath was hard, and though bringing justice to those who no longer had a voice was satisfying, seeing the spot a person's life had been snuffed out was one part of my job I could live without.

I was standing in Caroline's living room, glancing at a wall full of photographic memories that gave the impression of a person who had lived a boisterous, full life. Only now, aside from the faint hum of the refrigerator, the rooms were quiet, the radio switched off, the photos left to grow old, gathering dust and living a life Caroline wouldn't. Standing there, absorbing the stale stillness, I understood why James kept Grace away. A place once warm and bright felt cold and indifferent now. There was nothing for her here, nothing for her to come back to, not anymore.

I packed up Grace's closet and hauled the boxes to the car he had loaned me to drive during my time in the city. It was a black

BMW 8 Series coupe that handled so well, I was thinking of switching out my ride when I got back home.

If there was an obvious clue to be found in Caroline's house, I wasn't finding it. Most of the items that remained served a functional purpose in one way or another. Caroline's minimalist decor made her place easy to search but provided no clues or leads relating to the cause of her murder. Discouraged, I ended my search in Caroline's bedroom. The white furnishings were feminine and elegant, just like she had been in the photos I'd seen—a tall woman with long, auburn hair and big, bright eyes, who looked much younger than her actual age.

I browsed the dresser drawers and then picked apart her closet, striking out yet again. A large, dark-blue rug on the floor caught my eye. It was crooked and out of place, and the only disjointed item in the room. I peeled back the corner, finding what I knew I would beneath—dried bloodstains—making me wonder if James had repositioned the rug to mask the horrific events that had occurred such a short time ago.

At the far corner of the room was a mirrored jewelry cabinet. I walked over and opened it, staring at the delicate pieces of thin, gold jewelry hanging on the top two shelves. At the bottom of the cabinet were two drawers. I slid the top one open. It contained a variety of rings. A few bracelets occupied the second drawer, but it was what I found below the bracelets that interested me. A pamphlet had been folded a couple of times until it was reduced to the size of a small notepad. It had then been placed beneath the bracelets. I pulled it out and opened it, staring at a black-and-white photo of a man on the front. His name was Evan Hall, and he looked to be in his late thirties. The pamphlet was his obituary.

Evan had passed away a few months earlier, although the cause of death was not explained. Caroline was listed on the inside as one of the speakers at his funeral. I refolded the pamphlet and stuck it inside my purse. As I was shutting the cabinet door, I caught a glimpse of movement outside. I jerked my head toward the bedroom window, canvassing the area beyond the pool.

Could the palm trees swaying in the tropical breeze have been what I thought I'd seen? Or had it been something different?

Downstairs, the front door creaked open, a door I had firmly closed upon entry. I was no longer alone. *Someone* was there with me. On instinct, I reached inside my bag and then I remembered I wasn't at home. I was in Australia. I had no gun and no weapon. I scanned the room, looking for anything I could use to defend myself, but there wasn't time. The sound of footsteps ascending the stairs and shuffling down the hall toward me meant one thing—in a few seconds, I'd be out of time.

I hid behind the bedroom door and grabbed my cell phone out of my pocket. Hands trembling, I managed to send a short text to James: *Someone in sister's house. Help.* Through the crack in the bedroom door, I could see a figure turn to enter the room, but it had moved too fast for me to ascertain whether I was dealing with a man or a woman. I waited until the person had fully walked into the room, and then I sprung out from behind the door, wrapping my arm around the intruder's neck and pulling back, a move I'd learned years earlier in jiu-jitsu. I tightened my grip, intending to render the assailant unconscious, but then my eyes came to rest on the head attached to the neck I was squeezing, and I flicked my hands back and let go.

The head of hair was thin and curly and *gray.*

And *I* was an imbecile.

The elderly woman pressed her hands to her throat and bent down, gagging.

"I'm so sorry," I said. "Are you okay? Can I get you something … water … or—"

She whipped around, stabbing a finger into my chest. "What in the living hell is wrong with you? You just about killed me, you stupid, stupid woman!"

"I thought you were a—"

"Oh, no, you didn't. You didn't *think* at all."

"Who are you?" I asked.

"Adelaide Wiggins. I live across the street. *Who* are *you*?"

"My name is Sloane Monroe. James sent me here to pick up some of Grace's clothes."

"Is that so? What are you doing snooping around Caroline's bedroom, then? Grace's clothes are in *Grace's* room, not in here."

My phone vibrated. Adelaide stared at the name of the caller on the screen, ripped the phone from my hands, and answered it.

"James, it's Adelaide. Do you know a headstrong, silly bird named Sloane? Did you send her here? She says you sent her here. Is that true? Because if it isn't, I'm in danger, and I'll need you to hang up and call the police."

The woman had a flare for the dramatic and an even bigger need for attention, it seemed. James confirmed we knew each other and asked her to put me on the phone.

Through a hissed, frustrated breath, she said, "Fine, but if I have any injuries, one of you is getting a bill."

She shoved the phone into my hand and sat on Caroline's bed, hissing her disdain for me and crossing her arms in front of her.

I pressed the phone to my ear. "Sorry for the false alarm. I heard someone in the house and thought it was an intruder."

"No worries," he said. "You did what you should have done. Adelaide can be a lot to deal with sometimes. Are you all right?"

"I'm fine. I'm just a little shaken up. Let me speak to Adelaide for a minute, and I'll call you back when I leave here."

I ended the call and turned toward her. "Before you entered the house, were you standing by the hedges in the back yard, watching me through the bedroom window?"

She narrowed her eyes, looking at me as though I was heavily medicated.

"Why would I be spying on you through windows in the back garden?" she said. "I came through the front door, just like I always do."

"You could have knocked."

"Whatever for? I never had to knock when Caroline was alive. Why should I start now?"

I couldn't stop thinking about what I might have seen outside.

"Excuse me for a minute," I said. "I need to check on something."

I brushed past her, opening the door leading from Caroline's room to the back yard.

"Well now, just wait a minute," she called after me. "Where are you going in such a hurry?"

I ignored the question.

Aside from a variety of birds enjoying a sunny day in the tropics, I appeared to be alone. I glanced in the direction I thought I'd seen movement before. If someone had been there, they weren't anymore. Or perhaps no one had been there, and my habit of overthinking everything had reared its ugly head.

Adelaide walked outside and stood beside me. "*Now* what are you doing?"

"Before you came into the house, I could have sworn someone was back here."

Hands on hips, she glanced around. "Well, no one is here now, and I doubt anyone was here earlier. People in this neighborhood have been running scared ever since those two were killed, and I can't understand why. The killer won't strike here again. If he decides to kill again, he'll move to new ground."

"What makes you think so?"

"I watch those crime shows. Only an idiot would return to the same place twice. That's just asking to get caught, in my opinion."

It depended on the idiot. Serial "idiots" had a strange fascination with reliving the murder by returning to the place it happened. But I wasn't interested in engaging her in a debate. Not after what I'd just put her through.

"Grace came to your house the night her mother was killed," I said.

Adelaide nodded. "She did. Never seen a girl so scared as she was that night. She kept repeating herself, babbling on about her mum on the floor surrounded in blood. It's just so crazy, isn't it? She escapes that house and minutes later, Hugh gets murdered too. Lunatic who killed them must have been sitting there, lurking in the shadows, waiting. It's any wonder she made it out alive. Poor thing. Her life is challenging enough. She didn't deserve the hell she's gone through."

"Challenging because she has Down syndrome?"

"That too, but also because she's a teenager, and she's just learning what being her age is all about."

"Did something happen to Grace recently?" I asked.

"She had her little heart broken."

"How?"

"Grace became friends with a boy at school this year named Tommy Walker. She was sweet on him, and as far as I could tell, he felt the same way she did. It was cute, seeing the two of them together. She loves cheese pizza, and he used to bring a box around, and they'd sit on the front porch, laughing and carrying on. One day, Caroline looked out the window to check on them, and she saw Tommy give Grace a kiss. It was innocent enough, but Caroline sent Tommy home straightaway. She told him he couldn't come back—not for a while, at least. Broke Grace's heart. Caroline was always a tad overprotective when it came to Grace. Guess I couldn't blame her, though."

"When did this happen?"

Adelaide glanced to the side, thinking. "Oh, about three months ago or so, I'd say."

"Did you ever see Tommy at the house after Caroline told him not to come around?"

She shook her head. "As far as I know, they only saw each other at school."

"You seem to know a lot about Grace."

"I do know a lot about her. She used to come over sometimes after school, and we would watch *Mastermind Australia*. You ever see it?"

"I haven't."

Adelaide shook her head. "You're missing out. It's a game show. They ask trivia questions. It's kind of like that show you have in the States. You know the one. What's it called?"

"*Who Wants to Be a Millionaire?*"

"Oh, no. It's much more intense than that. Let me see now. I believe it's called *Jeopardy*."

"Have you seen anyone suspicious at the house since the murders happened?" I asked.

She winked. "Besides you, you mean? No. I haven't."

"What did you think about Caroline's boyfriend, Hugh?"

"Seemed all right. You're asking a lot of questions for someone who just popped around to pick up Grace's clothes. How do you know James, anyway? Are you two dating or something?"

"I'm married."

She shrugged. "So what?"

"I met James on my last visit to Australia. It was the week he was supposed to be married. I knew one of the bridesmaids."

Adelaide leaned in and lowered her voice, even though no one else was around. "That was some nasty business. Rumor was he called his wedding off because his fiancée had an affair the week of the wedding. Back when all this was going on, I'd asked Caroline about it, but she wouldn't give me any details. Is it true? Did his fiancée have an affair? She's a complete arse if she did. That man's as steamy as one of those Fifty Shades novels."

"It's not my place to talk about it."

She nodded. "Right. Better you didn't, then."

"Do you know of anyone who wanted to harm Caroline?"

"It's like I told the police. Caroline was a good person, well-respected in the community. Everyone seemed to like her. But you never know about people. There's a lot of crazy in the world today. Can't be too careful."

On this single topic, we agreed.

She glanced at her watch, gasped, and then bolted toward the back gate. "Oh, my. Look at the time. I have to get going. I have a meat pie on the counter that needs to be put into the oven. Nice meeting you."

CHAPTER 11

Adelaide headed back to her house, leaving me deep in thought about the conversation we'd just had and where to take my investigation next. Caroline's office seemed like the most logical idea, and I hoped I'd get lucky somehow. On the way to the car, I couldn't stop thinking about what I thought I saw in the backyard and why the troublesome feeling I had was lingering, even now. It had *felt* like someone was there, camouflaging himself behind the shrubbery. I couldn't shake how real it seemed.

Something else was bothering me too. Tommy Walker. I wondered how he'd felt after being told he was banned from seeing Grace at the house. If he had been angry with Caroline about being sent away, was it possible his anger was enough to drive him to kill? And why hadn't James spoken of him?

Although I didn't relish the idea of spending more time with Adelaide, she seemed adept at knowing everyone's business. I wondered if she would know who Evan Hall was and where Tommy Walker lived. Figuring it was worth an extra five minutes of my time to ask, I crossed the street and headed to her house for answers.

Adelaide's front door was slightly ajar when I reached it. Not comfortable walking in like she'd just walked in on me, I tapped on the door screen.

"Adelaide?" I said. "It's Sloane. I have a couple questions I forgot to ask you before."

If she heard me, she gave no indication of it. A television was on somewhere inside. The volume was high enough that it may have masked my voice. I called out to her again, louder this time.

Still nothing.

I tried the latch on the door. It was open. I walked inside.

"Adelaide. It's Sloane. I'm coming in."

I followed the foyer to the kitchen and glanced around. The oven was on. The meat pie she'd come home to fuss over was still resting on the counter. Dishes were soaking on the left side of the sink, and the faucet was running on the right. I switched it off. I turned around, and my shoes squeaked. I glanced down, seeing a few splotches of water across the floor next to the mat in front of the sink.

For a woman who looked to be in her eighties, she appeared sharp and intelligent, like there wasn't much in life that got past her. Intelligent people didn't leave their faucet running and their front door unlocked. Even in a place as safe as Cairns.

I entered the living room. She wasn't there. I grabbed the remote control to the television and pressed the mute button. I walked through the house, calling her name, but there was no sign of her anywhere.

In the bedroom, a plant had tipped over, and the terra-cotta pot had shattered onto the tile floor, scattering soil everywhere. The sliding glass door to the backyard was open. I stepped outside and spotted a torn piece of fabric resting on the grass. I picked it up and recognized it. It was from the orange-and-white floral dress Adelaide had been wearing. A stain in the corner of the fabric was red and wet. I rubbed a finger across it and then held the finger in front of me.

I was almost positive it was blood.

I took out my phone and dialed.

When James answered, I said, "I stopped at Adelaide's for a minute on my way out, and I can't find her. I think something's wrong."

"Why?" he said. "What's going on?"

"We were talking at Caroline's house, and she said she needed to put a pie in the oven. She left. About ten minutes later, I walked to her house to ask her a few more questions. The pie was still sitting on the counter, both doors to the house were open, the kitchen faucet was running, and a plant in her room is scattered all over the floor. And that's not all. Outside on the grass, I found a piece of fabric from the dress she was wearing. There's a red stain on it. It looks like blood."

"I'll call the police," he said. "Get out of there, Sloane. Right now."

"I'm not leaving. I need to know what happened to her."

"Until we know one way or another, you need to leave."

"I appreciate your concern, but I'm staying. Call the police. I'll get back to you when I know something."

I ended the call and headed toward the side of the house. Rounding the corner, I found the rest of the dress. A vast majority was soaked in blood.

Adelaide was dead.

CHAPTER 12

Eavesdropping without getting caught had always been something the man had excelled at. As a child, he'd hated it when his mum put him to bed earlier than she should have so she could watch movies with Uncle Frank in the living room. His father worked late as a nighttime construction supervisor. But his mum was predictable, and her ritualistic mannerisms were almost robotic and rarely changed. On those early bedtimes, she would put him to bed, wait ten minutes, and then check on him. If she thought he was asleep, she wouldn't return again until she retired for the night a few hours later. It took practice to create a believable illusion, but over time, he'd learned how to change his breathing pattern just enough to make it appear he was sleeping, even though he was wide awake.

Uncle Frank was his father's brother, and he liked to drink beer, especially on Sunday. For a long time, he'd stopped by on Sunday morning with a twelve-pack of Corona Extra, and by noon, he'd have consumed all of them while his mum polished off a bottle or two of wine. Then they'd sober up for the afternoon, go for a swim in the pool, and start in again after dinner.

The man hadn't minded his uncle coming around because his uncle made his mum laugh, and most of the time when his uncle wasn't there, she seemed melancholy and depressed. She'd say things like, "I hate my life," or "I wish I had money so I could get the hell out of here." As a child, he'd always thought it was his fault that she was unhappy, so he'd tried extra hard to be a good boy. But no matter how good he was, it never made a difference.

Then one night, everything changed. He'd snuck out of bed and tiptoed down the stairs to the fifth step down on the staircase. It was the perfect one because it allowed him to see what was going on in the living room but still be able to get back to his room in a hurry if his mum decided to head upstairs earlier than scheduled.

What he saw that night had startled him.

It was something he wasn't supposed to see—something he wished he'd *never* seen—his mum sitting on Uncle Frank's lap. And she wasn't just sitting … they were kissing.

When their lips parted, his uncle looked at his mum and said, "I'm going to take you out of here, take you away from all this. We'll start a new life in a new place and leave the past behind. Just you and me, baby."

Just you and me?

Just YOU and ME?

What about him?

Surely his mum would never leave without him.

Would she?

Trembling and worried, he'd watched the tears stream from his mum's eyes as she stared at his uncle and said, "Let's not wait until next month. Let's go, Frank. Let's go tomorrow. Can we? Please?"

But the tomorrow she'd hoped for would never come, not in the way she expected.

The next day, he'd gone hiking with his father and uncle in the rainforest. It was a quiet day—so quiet they'd only passed one other couple on the trail. After a while, they came to a lookout point, one that allowed them to look down and see across the ocean. His uncle held up a camera to snap a photo, but before he could take it, he slipped on a patch of loose pebbles. His father leaned down to help Uncle Frank, but he was too late. Uncle Frank slid over the side, smacking his head against a boulder, his body tossing and turning like a ragdoll as it tumbled down the rocky ravine.

The fall had killed his uncle instantly.

That's what his father had told the police, at least.

His dad had said it was an accident—a horrible, unfortunate accident.

Only it hadn't been.

He'd watched his father reach for his uncle. But instead of grabbing him and pulling him to safety like he could have done, his father did something else.

He *pushed* him.

When news of Uncle Frank's death reached his mum, she'd locked herself in her room, sobbing. She emerged the following day, saying she was going for a swim in the pool. At the time no one had noticed the empty bottle of pills she'd left on the dresser. Twenty minutes later she was found dead, floating facedown in the pool. And he was the one who'd found her.

The man had never been fond of pools after that day—or hiking, for that matter. An hour earlier when he'd sat in silence behind the shrubs surrounding Caroline's pool, trying to listen to the conversation between the foreigner and Caroline's neighbor, the pool had been so distracting, he had to squeeze his eyes shut and silently count to ten to calm his nerves and stop the flashes of horrific memories of the last day he'd seen his mum alive.

When his mind calmed, he'd overheard the foreigner asking a lot of questions, just like she had the day before in the park. Even if she had met the senator right before his wedding, it didn't explain what she was doing back here now or why she was so damn nosy. And before the neighbor arrived, he watched the foreigner snoop around Caroline's room.

What was she doing?

The old woman had talked to the foreigner about Caroline and the night of the murders. Some of what she said was factual. Other details were lies, which angered the man. He was tired of false truths and false people, and as the weeks since Caroline's death ticked by one thing was becoming clear: something had to be done.

CHAPTER 13

Fifteen minutes earlier, Adelaide and I had been talking in Caroline's back yard. Now she was face up in the center of her flower garden, dead. I called for an ambulance. When the call ended, a feeling swept over me, the same feeling I'd had before at Caroline's house. My eyes darted around. I saw no one, but it didn't mean the killer wasn't there, hiding, as I believed he had been before.

In the most stable, confident voice I could muster at a time like this, I said, "If you're here, why don't you come out and face me? Don't be a coward."

I wasn't sure I was ready for a confrontation, but if he was there, I was better off knowing where he was and what I was up against. A flickering motion in the bushes sent shockwaves through my veins. I whipped around and pressed a hand to my chest, taking a lengthy, much-needed breath.

Calm yourself, Sloane. It's only a butterfly. He's probably gone now.

And he may have been, but he'd left a noticeable signature for all to see. The knife he likely used as the murder weapon had been stabbed upright into a mound of soil next to Adelaide's body like the sword in the stone. Leaving it behind was bold and sent a message of its own—only this time it wasn't the only one. Across Adelaide's forehead, a single word was written in a dark shade of red. From its texture, I could tell it wasn't blood. It was waxy, like lipstick, and given the humidity of the day, it was melting.

The word was LIAR.

Assuming the word wouldn't remain intact until the police arrived. I snapped a photo and sent it to James. Then I stood there, staring down at Adelaide, wondering what she had lied about, or if she'd lied at all, and if the killer had falsely accused her as part of what seemed to be becoming an evolving game.

Could there have been any truth to his accusation?

If she *had* lied, had it been to me?

The sound of a vehicle skidding to a stop in the driveway diverted my attention. Thinking it was the ambulance, I walked into the front yard but was met by two police officers instead.

The taller of the two said, "Are you the woman who called for an ambulance?"

I nodded.

"Who are you?" he continued. "And why are you here?"

I told him. Well, I didn't *tell* him, tell him. I casually mentioned I was in Australia to visit with James.

The two officers exchanged glances, and the shorter one said, "Where is Adelaide Wiggins?"

I pointed. "Over there in the flower garden on the side of the house."

The shorter one requested backup, and the tall one told me to stay put and not to go anywhere. A minute later, James arrived, followed by Victoria, followed by the ambulance. Victoria offered a slight smile and nodded at me as she speed-walked past, which I understood. She was there to do a job, and it was better for her to act like we were nothing more than acquaintances, which, for the most part, we were.

James tilted his head toward the back of the yard, indicating he wanted me to follow him. I did. We reached the edge of the property, and in a lowered voice, he said, "The police are going to have a lot of questions. Let me handle it, all right?"

"I'm not worried," I said. "I can answer their questions. They know I exist now, and telling them I stopped by after grabbing some clothes for Grace shouldn't seem that suspicious."

"To them, *everything* is suspicious, and when you're questioned, they'll want to know everything about you—who you are, why you're here, and maybe even what you know about the case. If by some miracle they don't look into you further, we need to keep the private-investigator part to ourselves, for now. Understand? I'm not asking you to lie. I'm asking you to be vague with the details you offer."

I nodded. "I've dealt with the cops for years. I know what to say. It might go better if you're with me when I give my statement, though."

"I will be. I just want you to be prepared for what's coming."

I was on the fence about whether or not to tell the police what I did as a career. By withholding it, if they *did* decide to look me up—and I assumed they would—it would appear like I was deliberately trying to keep something from them. Then again, being upfront about it so early on in the case could make matters worse and derail my chances of remaining involved.

More police arrived, and the tall officer approached me and said I needed to go to the station so they could take my statement.

He said, "You can come with me. I'll take you over."

The idea didn't bode well with James.

"That's not necessary," James said. "I'll take her."

The tall officer frowned and said, "Fine, Senator Ashby. You two should head over now, though."

James nodded, and we walked to the car. On the way, he glanced back at Victoria like he was hoping he'd have the chance to say goodbye before we left. She was too busy assessing Adelaide to notice anything else going on around her ... or to see the smile on his face when he gazed at her, something he hadn't done much of since I arrived.

Once we got to the car, he handed me a folded piece of paper.

"What's this?" I asked.

"My dad's number."

"Why?"

"You *know* why. If you need him, for anything, for any reason, and you can't reach me, I want you to give him a call, okay?"

I nodded, even though I wasn't sure his dad would be in favor of the idea.

"There are a few things you should know about the way things work around here," he said. "Police can't force you to go to the station unless you've been arrested. You're going in of your own free will, which is good. You're cooperating. Legally they can question you for up to four hours. In that time, you can answer the questions they ask, or you can refuse. Your choice. I'd suggest answering whatever you can unless it's something you shouldn't be answering. My lawyer is meeting us there, and he'll assist with the finer details. *He* knows why you're here."

"You called your lawyer? Why? Seems a bit extreme if they're only taking a statement. Don't you think I'll look like I have something to hide?"

"Not necessarily. When they ask why he's there, I'll explain I called him to represent you because you're not from around here, aren't familiar with the way things work in these situations, or about your rights, and he's offered to help you through it. Leave it with me. It will all be fine."

I told myself there was nothing to be concerned about.

I told myself not to worry, that everything would be all right.

I just wish I believed it.

CHAPTER 14

James' lawyer was waiting at the station when we arrived. He was around my height, five-eight, and looked to be mid-forties, somewhere around my age. What he lacked in inches he made up for in a lion's mane of blonde hair that had been combed back into a neat ponytail and a body that was dating the gym on a regular basis. We approached him, and he stuck his hand out toward me.

"Hi, Sloane. It's good to meet you. I'm Charles Branson, but everyone around here calls me Charlie."

His handshake was even firmer than his biceps.

"I assumed you would be Australian," I said, "but you're not."

"There's a lot more diversity in this city than most people who aren't from here realize. I'm from Great Britain, but I've been here for eleven years."

"What made you come here?"

"I came as a backpacker. I stayed because I prefer the weather over here to the weather at home, for starters."

James patted Charlie on the shoulder. "And the people. You like them too. Go on … admit it."

Charlie grinned. "Some more than others."

James turned toward me. "I have an errand to run."

"I thought you said you'd be doing this with me?" I said.

"Charlie represents me, so in a way, it's like I'm still here. I'll be back to pick you up."

"It's fine," I said. "I can grab a taxi back to my hotel."

"After the police are done with you, I'd like to go over everything that happened with Adelaide. I know it's a lot, but on the car ride over, there wasn't time to get through it. I'll swing by to get you, and we can grab dinner. Sound okay?"

I nodded. After blowing him off the day before, I wasn't about to balk at his suggestion by telling him how much I'd been looking forward to unwinding, pouring myself a glass of wine, and soaking in the hot tub in my hotel room later.

I spent the next couple of hours in a boxy, humid room providing details about my short-lived time with Adelaide. Charlie stayed quiet for the most part, only interjecting to say things like, "She answered that already," and "I don't see how this is relevant to the case," and "Can we move on?"

By the time we finished, I figured he'd be soaking in a hot tub of his own later.

When the police seemed satisfied they had sucked all of the information they could out of me, I was thanked for my time and told I could go, a process which was far more pleasant than those I'd experienced at police stations in the past.

I found James waiting for me outside.

"How did it go in there?" he asked.

"I think they suspect I'm here as more than just your friend who's visiting to help you through a tough time, but I could be wrong."

I wasn't wrong, but I didn't want to further complicate things until they complicated themselves. For now, I hoped the police had far more to deal with than figuring me out.

We drove to an Italian place named Coltello e Forchetta, which James said was Italian for "knife and fork." It was part restaurant and part bar, and tonight it was quiet, which suited us perfectly.

We sat at the bar, ordered a couple of appetizers, and a bottle of Shiraz to share.

"How's Grace?" I asked. "Does she know about Adelaide?"

"Not yet. We're trying to keep her away from the news for as long as we can. She was quite fond of Adelaide. The news of her death won't be easy for her, but then, nothing is right now."

His cell phone buzzed. He looked at the text message on the screen, typed a reply, and then slid the phone into his pocket. "Victoria just let me know she has returned to the lab and will be staying late to see what she can find. She's started processing Adelaide, but so far, everything is straightforward. Single stab wound to the chest, similar in entry point to Caroline's."

"Is Victoria alone at the lab?"

"Her assistant is with her, and there's an officer just inside the door. After this latest attack, they're not taking any chances. They've suggested sending a couple officers to my place as well. I appreciate their consideration, but I'd rather they look out for everyone else."

"But you have Grace, and you're not always there."

"I know. That's why I gave them the go-ahead to come over, even though they would have whether they had my permission or not."

I thought back to the events of the day. "I believe the killer saw me today at Caroline's place. When I was in her bedroom, I thought I saw someone by the pool. I went outside and didn't see anyone, but after what happened to Adelaide, I'm sure it was him."

"That brings me to my next point," he said. "I don't like the thought of you staying at the hotel. You should stay at my place tonight. I have a guesthouse out back, a surveillance system in place, and the police watching the house now, as you know. You'd have your privacy, and you'd also be protected."

The burning question was … did it have a hot tub?

I preferred to stay on my own, without the pressure of feeling like I needed to check in with anyone when I wanted to come and go, but I understood his concern, and even though I didn't mind a moderate amount of risk, the idea of being safe was appealing too.

"I'll think about it," I said.

He placed a hand on my arm. "It would make me feel better. I brought you into this, thinking only of my own personal interest in wanting my sister's murder to be solved. It's turned into more than that, much more. This maniac could be on a killing spree. We have no idea what he's thinking. Stay at my place tonight, and I'll send you back to the States tomorrow."

"No, you won't. I'm not going anywhere."

"I won't risk something happening to you. I don't want to lose anyone else."

"My job is dangerous," I said. "It always has been. If I go home, I'll take another job just as risky. You'd be protecting me from one madman and pushing me into the arms of another. You'd also be taking away my choice of whether to stay or not, and I'm not going anywhere."

The bartender placed the wineglasses in front of us and poured. James raised his glass and clanked it against mine saying, "You're a strong-willed woman, Sloane. May you be safe—in this endeavor, and in whatever else comes your way in life."

We drank to my longevity and then set the glasses back on the counter.

"I'm still trying to understand what the killer wrote on Adelaide's forehead," I said. "He labeled her a liar. Any idea what he thinks she's lying about?"

James tapped a finger on the counter and stared into his glass. "Could be any number of things. I knew Adelaide, but I didn't know her well. What did the two of you talk about in the back garden? If he was there, listening, maybe he heard something he didn't like."

I thought about the conversation we'd had. "She did make a few derogatory comments about the killer."

"Like what?"

"She said only an idiot would return to the same place twice. She also called him a lunatic."

"What else?"

"We talked about Grace fleeing to her house that night, and the possibility the killer may have still been at the house at the time, since Hugh wasn't dead yet. Adelaide also asked if your wedding was called off because of an affair. I didn't answer the question."

He shook his head. "I'm not surprised she'd probe you about it. She was one of the nosiest people I've ever met. Anything else?"

"She told me about Tommy Walker. He's actually the reason I went to her house after she left. I wanted to ask if she had his address so I could talk to him. You haven't mentioned him to me. Why not?"

"He's a bit of a thorn in my side at the moment."

"In what way?"

James drank the rest of the wine in his glass and poured himself another. "He's called my office several times asking to see Grace. I keep pawning him off on my secretary."

"Why won't you speak to him?"

"I have no idea what to *do* about him yet. I've never had a teenager, and I've never been in this situation. I was hoping he'd stop calling, but he hasn't, and now I have Grace pressuring me to allow her to see him too."

"It sounds like they were close. Why won't you let her see him? It might do her some good."

He shook his head. "Until the killer is caught, I trust very few people at the moment. Even him. He seems to be a good kid, or at least he appears to be one, but nothing is as it seems right now, is it?"

"Does Tommy have Down syndrome too?"

He nodded. "They go to the same school. As far as I know, the kid's been good for Grace. This last year, she's been happier than I've ever seen her before. I believe he has a lot to do with it."

"Wouldn't it help her to see him, then? You could be there to supervise."

"I just can't allow it ... not right now."

I understood the urge he had to be an overprotective uncle, given there was a killer running amok in the city, and Grace had a lot of healing still to do. But isolating her from those she cared about seemed extreme. Then again, I didn't know Tommy, and I didn't have children, either. Maybe James' concern was valid.

"I guess I'm trying to work out why the killer committed two murders, then had a cooling-off period, and then made the decision to kill Adelaide," I said. "And I can't decide if the murders were premeditated, if they were crimes of passion, or if they were something else entirely. What do you think?"

He shrugged. "I'm with you. It's hard to say."

"In the months before Caroline was killed, was anyone else murdered?"

"Murder isn't common in Cairns. In fact, it hardly exists. Before Caroline and Hugh, there hadn't been a murder in the last four years, and even then, it was open and shut."

"What happened?"

"It was a marital dispute between a husband and wife. He smacked her in the back of the head with a shovel and cracked her skull open. She died, and he's still behind bars. What we're dealing with now ... it's different."

I dug into my purse, shuffling things around until I found the obituary I'd taken. I pulled it out and showed it to him. "This was inside your sister's jewelry case. Do you know him or who he was to her?"

James glanced at the pamphlet. "Evan Hall was one of Caroline's patients. I accompanied her to his funeral."

"What happened to him?"

"He committed suicide. He hung himself with a belt in the living room of his house. Beyond that, I don't know much. No one at the funeral discussed any details about why it happened, and when I asked Caroline, she was vague too. She wouldn't even tell me anything about his treatment protocol."

"If Evan was no longer alive, it's not like she needed to keep those details from you. Did you ask her why she wouldn't talk about it?"

"Even in death, she felt the need to respect his privacy. It was important to her, so I never pressured her to say more. I always had the feeling his death affected her, though."

"In what way?" I asked.

"She seemed down in the weeks after he passed and not like her usual bubbly self. She never said her altered mood had anything to do with him, but I believe it did."

He was her former patient, a person she'd been tasked with trying to help. I expect she may have felt like in some ways, she'd let him down.

"I assume you've been through her office," I said. "Did you find anything of interest?"

He nodded. "She kept her client list on her laptop, and the police have that. I don't know what they've done with it, other than telling me they've been going through the list and questioning everyone."

"What about her notes? She should have kept written information about what went on in her sessions."

"She did. I remember seeing her notebook from time to time. She always stuck it in the back compartment of her handbag. It wasn't there though. I checked. It wasn't in her office, either."

"What about any notebooks she used in the past?"

"None of them have been found."

"Strange, don't you think?" I said.

"It didn't concern me at first. But the more I've thought about it, the more I have started to think there may be some reason as to why they seem to be missing."

"You said she was private about her patients, but did she ever speak in general terms or hypotheticals?"

"How do you mean?"

"Did she ever have a problem with a patient and discuss it with you without mentioning the patient's name?"

He shook his head. "Never. All I can tell you is that she loved what she did, and she cared about each and every person she was trying to help. Knowing she made a difference in the lives of those she worked with made her feel fulfilled in a way I don't think anything else ever did."

"Did she specialize in any particular area?"

"She treated a wide variety of issues and illnesses, but anxiety, depression, and past trauma were her main areas of focus, where she felt she could make the biggest difference."

I ran my hands up and down my arms. For as warm as it was in the tropics, the restaurant's air conditioning made it feel like a Park City ski resort in the dead of winter.

"You're cold," he said.

"I'm okay."

He stood. "I have a sweater in the car. I'll grab it for you."

I scooted my chair back. "It's really okay. Maybe we should get going. Won't Grace be waiting for you?"

"She's out to dinner with my dad tonight and won't be home for a few more hours. Sitting here, talking with you, sharing a bottle of wine, even after what happened to Adelaide earlier … I feel like I'm breathing for the first time today. I'd like to stay a while longer, if you don't mind. Not too long, thirty minutes or so. Sound good?"

There was still almost a half of a bottle of wine left, and in the time we'd been sitting at the bar, day had turned to night. I figured my investigation skills were just as well served sitting here, picking his brain, as they would be anywhere else.

"Sure, we can stay," I said.

James headed outside while I remained at the bar, sipping my wine and pondering my agenda for tomorrow. I still knew little about the killer. With no hard clues as to his motive, I was unsure which direction I should go next. I also thought about what I'd do when I found him. I was without a way to protect myself, visiting a country where I wasn't able to carry my gun—or *any* gun for that matter.

Down Under, it was illegal to carry anything intended for use as a weapon. This included guns, knives, tasers, and even non-deadly forms of protection like pepper spray. Coming from a country where owning a firearm was second nature to most people if they chose to have one, I wondered if Australians felt safer without weapons. Or not. In my thirties I'd practiced jiu-jitsu, advancing high enough to be considered a weapon in my own right. Still, without any other way to defend myself, I felt vulnerable and naked. The killer was apparently armed with an array of knives.

I had nothing.

I poured myself a quarter glass of wine and stared at a clock shaped like a wallaby on the wall behind the bar. Twelve minutes had passed since James had gone to the car. In my estimation, it shouldn't have taken more than five to get there and back. Maybe he was on the phone. Or maybe he wasn't. Sitting there, watching time tick by, I became consumed with what could be keeping him, and my anxiety spun into overdrive.

Wondering wouldn't suffice.

To satisfy myself, I needed to know why he hadn't returned yet, and I needed to know now.

While the bartender handed a drink to a customer on the opposite end of the counter, I leaned over the bar, plucking one of the knives he'd been using to slice limes. I tucked it into my purse and stood up, looking at the clock once again.

Fourteen minutes had come and gone.

Something wasn't right.

CHAPTER 15

I headed out of the restaurant, sprinting toward James' car. The driver's-side door was open, the interior light was on, and his cell phone was sitting on the seat. The sweater he'd meant to bring me was still on the back seat where he'd left it. And James was nowhere to be seen.

I spun around, my eyes darting back and forth, scanning the area. "James, are you out here? James! Where are you?"

A couple walking hand in hand across the parking lot stared at me like they thought I was intoxicated. The man gripped the woman's hand tighter, and then they quickly changed direction, as if trying to get as far away from me as possible.

I braced myself against the car and breathed, trying to get my nerves under control. When I was able to focus again, my eyes came to rest on the car's windshield. A few letters were written across it in the same shade of red that I'd seen on Adelaide's forehead, only this time it said: FOO, a word clearly left unfinished.

I surmised James had caught the killer in the act of vandalizing his car before the killer had a finished product. If I was right, where was James? And where was the killer?

The restaurant was located at the far end of the pier where the cruise liners docked when they entered port. With one direction leading out to sea, three other possible directions to investigate remained, and that was *if* James was still in the area.

I needed help.

I palmed my cell phone, intending to call the police, but then I spotted James' watch several feet in front of me on the sidewalk. I rushed over and picked it up. The watch face had a small crack, and the sidewalk where it had been sitting was littered with what appeared to be blood spatter that continued into the park. I switched my cell phone's flashlight on and followed the droplets of blood into the park, where the grass hid them from view.

I glanced around. "James? Are you here?"

The sound of a man groaning washed through the trees. It was faint, but loud enough for me to confirm the direction it had come from. I raced through the darkness and found James bent over on all fours. He was bloody, but alive—for now.

I readied my kitchen knife and glanced around. Seeing no one, I dropped to my knees beside him.

"How bad are you hurt?" I asked.

He raised his body enough for me to see he'd been stabbed in at least two places—once in the hand, and the other in the abdomen. He attempted to lean against the tree and come to a sitting position, a move that proved to be a mistake. Blood was pouring from his chest more rapidly now. He was losing too much of it, too fast.

I pressed my hand over his, pushed into his chest, and said, "You're losing too much blood. We have to stop it. We have to keep applying pressure."

With my other hand, I thumbed the number to the police station. Before the call was answered, James' eyes closed and his body went limp, sagging to the ground next to me. When my call was picked up, I blurted, "I'm at the park across from Coltello e Forchetta. Senator James Ashby has been stabbed. I need someone here. Now!"

CHAPTER 16

I had always found the mind to be a complex curiosity, especially when multiple things all occurred at basically the same time. The overload often forced my mind into protection mode. I'd always assumed it was my brain's way of compartmentalizing, slowing down a situation riddled with too many moving parts to process in one given moment. When the parts became still enough to filter the rapid-fire events into internal boxes, then I could open and examine each one individually, instead of all at the same time.

My mental boxes of unfortunate events were stacked on top of each other, and as the seconds passed, I had started pulling them down, unpacking each detail until every box had been opened. I then tried blending them together into one, forcing myself to remember the pattern of events as they occurred so I didn't forget. At the moment, it proved to be an impossible task. My mind was an endless fog, and the more I tried to stitch the recent events of the night together, the more they kept unraveling.

I was alone in a hospital room on a bed, fully clothed, including my shoes, unsure of how I'd ended up there. My head was throbbing.

For all the things I *didn't* know, there were a few things I did:

1. James had tried to tell me something when I'd reached him, but he'd had trouble talking. His voice had been low and gravelly, and I had been too preoccupied trying to stop the blood from pouring out of his chest to understand a word he was saying.

2. My call to the police seemed to go on a lot longer than I remembered. When I checked my phone, I noticed the duration was four minutes, even though I was sure it had been closer to one.

3. I had started having flashbacks from the time after I'd called the police and before they arrived ... of someone else being in the park. I was on the ground looking up, staring up at what I assumed was a man, but his face was blurred to me. Whether he was real or something my mind had invented, I wasn't sure.

4. And finally, I had no idea where James had been taken and whether he was dead or alive.

CHAPTER 17

The foreigner had looked so peaceful resting on the ground next to the senator. With one flick of his wrist, the man could have easily slit her throat if he'd wanted to, and she would have been dead. But killing her hadn't appealed to him in that moment. He didn't have enough of a reason to rationalize her death. Not yet, anyway. And with the senator dead, the justice the man had been seeking had been served. He saw no point in adding to the death toll again unless he had to.

Over the last day, he'd spent a great deal of time pondering just how much killing was *too* much killing, or if the concept of a certain number making more of a difference than another actually mattered in the end. He'd come to a decision that it wasn't practical for murder to be viewed in terms of numbers, or in deciding how much killing was too much.

It was more of a matter of principle.

Some people *needed* to die.

Plain and simple.

And ridding the world of such filth made it a better place.

Every time he opened the paper or switched on the news and saw a crime go unpunished, it lit a fire inside him that refused to go out. Why did some crimes come with a heavy price, while others weren't deemed punishable at all? And why did only certain people have the ability to pass judgment on everyone else? Society as a whole seemed unfair and biased, something that needed to change.

And why was it so many murderers seemed to kill for pleasure? He took no pleasure in what he did. It was merely a way of exacting justice that wouldn't be served any other way.

A week earlier, he'd read an article outlining murder statistics around the world. He was pleased to learn Australia ranked 183 out of 216 countries. The United States was far worse, ranking at 111. But even America paled in comparison to Honduras, where over ninety percent of the murders in the world occurred per every hundred thousand residents.

Those lunatics were the *real* savages.

Not him.

He could kill a hell of a lot more if he wanted and not even make a dent in Honduras' outrageously high average. He could continue killing for the remainder of his life if he liked, and Australia would still never end up on top.

But did he want to?

Killing people was a lot of work, and it exhausted him, mentally and physically. Each time he forced a blade into someone's chest, there was a heaviness attached to it when he pulled it out. It was almost like taking the life of another stripped away years from his.

He'd done what he'd set out to do, and he'd gotten away with it. What was the point in continuing? There was a lot more to life than murder—like gourmet sauces and exotic cuisine, hobbies he'd once struggled at, but now mastered.

It had been a long, murderous day.

He stripped off his clothes, changed into a pair of plaid pajamas, and rested his head on a pillow, congratulating himself on a good night's work. He was so entranced in his thoughts he almost didn't notice Petey, who was sitting in a recliner chair next to the bed, reading a book.

"To kill or not to kill," the man said. "I don't know, Petey. What do you think?"

CHAPTER 18

James' father Noel—a.k.a. Froggy—entered my hospital room, crossed in front of my bed, and sat on a chair opposite me. He looked a lot paler today than he had the last time I saw him. He also looked worried, and I prepared for the worst.

He folded his arms in front of him and said, "How ya goin' today, Sloane?"

"All right, I think," I said. "But I'm not sure what's going on."

"I might be able to fill in the gaps for you."

I pushed a pillow behind me and sat up. "I wanted to apologize to you about how I behaved when we first met. I'd like to blame my behavior on jet lag, but there really was no excuse for it."

He shrugged. "No need to apologize. It's all good, darlin'. No worries."

"I shouldn't have been such a jerk to you, though. You didn't deserve it."

"Probably not, but it's all in the past now."

"How's James?" I asked. "I don't know what happened after I found him in the park. Is he …"

"Dead? No. Not yet."

"Not *yet?*"

"He's in surgery. I should know something in another hour or two. He's tough. Always has been. I expect he'll make it through and be all right, or maybe that's just what I keep telling myself because I've lost one child already. I'm not ready to lose another."

"What has the doctor said?"

"He couldn't believe James was still alive when he got here, because of all the blood he'd lost." He leaned back in the chair. "I've been thinking about the first time I stepped foot in this hospital. It was the day Caroline was born. She was such a little thing. Premature. Underweight. They kept her here for three weeks after she came into the world. Every day after I got off work, I'd drive over straightaway to see her. When I walked in and she looked up at me, I could swear I saw her eyes change, like she *knew* I'd be coming, like she'd been waiting all day for me to get there. Probably sounds crazy, but it's the truth."

"It doesn't sound crazy at all. Not to me."

"What made you decide to become a private investigator, if you don't mind me asking? Doesn't it wear on you? Isn't it hard spending your life surrounded by so much death all the time?"

"Death isn't all it is. It's just part of it."

"I guess I just don't understand what drives you to be in this line of work. Since Caroline died, I feel like I'm suffocating. All I want is to breathe like I used to, to feel normal again. I don't know if I ever will."

"You will, one day. You'll get there. It's a long process, but time offers the chance for healing."

"Are you speaking from experience?"

I nodded. "I am, but what I went through was different. I mean, same type of emotions, I suppose, but I can't imagine what it would be like to lose a child."

"I couldn't imagine it either, until it happened."

"James told me you're a retired chief superintendent."

"I am, but I'd say what I did and what you do on a routine basis are not the same. This city is a safe place, or it was until recently."

"I never thought I'd become a private investigator," I said. "I wanted to be a therapist."

"Then what made you decide to do it?"

"Several years ago, my sister was murdered, and her death changed everything."

His eyes widened, and he leaned forward. "How did it happen?"

"She was the victim of a serial killer named Sam Reids. He called himself 'Sinnerman.'"

"He still alive?"

I shook my head. "He's in the ground where he belongs."

"Hard to believe there are people in this world who are so evil. You kill him?"

"I wanted to," I said. "He was a real scumbag. I even had the chance, but I didn't go through with it. Someone else did it for me, so I didn't have to do it. Before we found the killer, I'd go into the police station at least once a week, checking in on any new leads they had. Even though they did everything they could to find him, any leads they had turned into dead ends. It was frustrating, for me and for them. I grew tired of feeling helpless and decided to learn everything I could about tracking murderers and getting inside their minds. I started working for a private detective agency that specialized in tougher cases, and I became good at it ... so good I opened a business of my own."

"You found Sinnerman?"

"I'd like to say I did," I said. "Truth is, he found *me* first."

"I've thought a lot about what I would do if I came face-to-face with the man responsible for all this—the man who has torn a hole through my family."

"I experienced the same feelings when it happened to me. In my situation, when we caught the guy, there was someone there with me. Someone who knew I'd never killed anyone before. He talked me out of doing the one thing I'd dreamed of doing since the day my sister drew her last breath. Ever since then all I've ever wanted to do is take on high profile cases like your daughter's and bring families the closure they're looking for."

"Do you only take on murder cases?"

I nodded. "I tried stopping for a while, tried taking other, less-risky jobs like internet searches on missing people, but it wasn't enough to satisfy me. Finding murderers is in my blood now. It makes me feel whole and alive. And now I suppose it's your turn to think *I* sound crazy."

He held two fingers up an inch apart from each other. "Maybe a little. You didn't kill the man responsible for your sister's death. Does that mean you've *never* killed anyone?"

"I do what it takes to get the job done. The person I was before, the one who went after Sam Reids, was more of a girl than a woman. I've changed a lot since then."

I grabbed the glass of water on the tray next to me and took a sip.

"Now you can answer something for me," I said.

"Sure. What would you like to know?"

"What the hell happened tonight?"

CHAPTER 19

W hen the police arrived at the park, they found you lying on the ground next to James," Noel said.

"I don't remember ever being on the ground," I said, "but I've been having flashbacks that suggest I was at one point."

"At first the paramedics thought you had been attacked too. Some parts of you were bloody. It wasn't your blood, though. It was James' blood. When they got you all cleaned up, there wasn't a mark on you. What do you remember?"

I still hadn't separated fact from fiction.

"I remember finding James," I said. "I put my hand on his chest to try to stop the bleeding. I'm just not sure what happened next."

"You called for help. Sometime during the call, the paramedics believe you passed out. Thankfully it wasn't long between your call and when the ambulance arrived."

"Why would I have passed out? I've been in far worse situations than this before."

"You didn't just faint once, darlin'. It happened a second time in the ambulance. You don't recall?"

I shook my head.

"You gave general information about James to the operator," he said, "and then it sounded like the line went dead, but the call was still engaged. The operator tried communicating with you several times, but you were unresponsive. Seems there's a lot you don't remember. What about the time frame before you found James?"

I crossed my arms, thinking. "After I exited the restaurant and realized James wasn't at the car, I found the watch he'd been wearing on the ground. There were spots of fresh blood on the sidewalk. The blood trail led me into the park where I found him."

"And was he alone?"

"Yes ... I mean ... I *think* so. I didn't *see* anyone else there, but I'm getting the feeling the killer likes hanging around in the shadows, watching what's going on. And I keep seeing glimpses in my mind of a man hovering over me, but I can't make out his face."

"Could have been the police or the paramedics."

Maybe, but my gut told me otherwise.

"James was stabbed in the chest, and it looked like his hand had been sliced too," I said. "Did he have any other injuries?"

"His upper left forearm was cut, but the wound wasn't deep. It's more of a scratch in comparison to the other ones."

"I wish I could have been there to help him."

Noel leaned forward and grabbed my hand. "You *were* there to help him, Sloane. You saved his life."

"I hope so."

"How did James end up in the park without you? Weren't you at the restaurant together?"

I nodded. "We'd ordered some wine and were talking about different things related to the case. He noticed I was cold and offered to get me the sweater he had in his car. He went outside to get it. Several minutes passed and he hadn't returned, so I went to check on him. I found the door to his car open, and … you know the rest."

"You see the letters written on the windshield?"

I nodded. "I'm not sure if the killer meant to attack James tonight. I believe his original plan may have been to vandalize James' car first, to send him a message. He could have been interrupted before he had the chance to write the last letter."

"We're all thinking the same thing."

"There aren't many words he could have been trying to write, given what he'd started with. 'Fool' is the obvious choice, especially since the killer called Adelaide a liar earlier today. What I don't understand is why Caroline's and Hugh's murders had no obvious signatures. Why mark some but not the others?"

"Hard to know the meaning of anything until we find the bastard."

"I have two possible theories on how James ended up in the park," I said. "The killer could have taken off when James spotted him, and James chased after him. The light in the park at night is a lot dimmer than the light in the parking lot. For the killer, that would have given him an advantage."

"Good theory. And the other one?"

"James ran toward the park, and the killer chased him."

"Why would he do that?"

"I don't know," I said. "I guess we'll find out when we get the chance to speak to James."

CHAPTER 20

My right shoe had been bugging me. My sock was all bunched up inside it, and I hadn't remembered tying the laces so tight. I removed my shoe to adjust the sock, and a silver gum wrapper fell out of the side. I picked it up, looking at how perfectly it had been folded down the middle. I was about to toss it out, when I noticed something odd—there appeared to be writing on the inside of the wrapper. I unfolded it, revealing the message: *Then the liars and swearers are fools, for there are liars and swearers enough to beat the honest men and hang up them.*

A few minutes earlier, I'd asked Noel to get me a cup of tea. He walked into the room, cup in hand, hesitating when he saw me scrutinizing the wrapper.

"What do you have there?" he asked.

"I knew it," I said. "I *knew* he was there."

"Knew *who* was there?"

"The killer."

He raised a brow. "How do you know for sure?"

I handed the wrapper to him. "This was folded up in my shoe. It's a quote from *Macbeth*."

Noel looked at me, confused.

"One of Shakespeare's plays."

"Oh, gotcha." Noel set the tea down next to me and held the wrapper in both hands, looking it over. "Writing is so small, I can barely read it without my glasses."

I read it aloud.

"I think the killer was there, hovering over me right before the ambulance arrived," I said. "He must have shoved the note inside my sock before he left. What kind of weirdo does something like that, knowing the police are on their way to the scene?"

"I think you're asking the wrong question."

"What's the right one?"

"He had the chance to kill you. Why didn't he?"

CHAPTER 21

It wasn't the first time I'd been at death's door, but it was my most vulnerable. Noel's question had rattled me to my core. If we were dealing with a cold-blooded killer, why had my life been spared when so many others hadn't? He had the opportunity to kill me and hadn't taken it.

Nothing made sense.

With my fainting spells showing no signs of returning, I was released from the room I'd been in at the hospital and relocated to the waiting area where I sat next to Noel, awaiting the outcome of James' surgery. It was a long hour and a half before the surgeon emerged and pulled Noel to the side. James was alive, having narrowly escaped death. If the knife he'd been stabbed with had been pushed in an inch further, as Caroline's had, James would be dead. James had a long way to go before he'd be back to himself again, but doctors believed, in time, he would make a full recovery.

I had appreciated Noel's sentiments about it being me who'd saved James' life, but I believed James had saved his own. He had defensive wounds on both hands, which caused the police to speculate the killer wasn't able to stab him as precisely as he intended.

As my memory returned, I had flashbacks of running through the park, screaming James' name. It was possible the killer heard me coming, and the distraction threw him off just enough to stop him from stabbing James again. At that point, I believed the killer assumed the blow he'd dealt James would prove fatal, and he fled the scene, remaining close by to watch events unfold.

The tall and short officers met me in the waiting room, and I handed over the wrapper I'd found in my shoe. As they bagged it, they began asking a series of questions but stopped when Victoria burst through the hospital's main entrance with a red, puffy face that looked like she'd been crying on the drive over. She noticed the officers and whipped around, blotting her eyes with the end of the shirt sleeve. She took a moment to compose herself and then walked over.

I grabbed hold of her arms and looked her in the eye. "He made it out of surgery, and the surgeon said the operation went well. It's a good sign. He'll be all right."

She showed signs of smiling, but then the tears began flowing again.

I turned to the taller of the two officers. "I need a few minutes."

"And we need answers to our questions," he said.

"You'll get them when I've finished talking to Victoria."

"We need them now."

I thought about pacifying him for exactly two seconds before deciding his lack of sympathy made me lack all consideration for his current needs.

"If you want my cooperation, you'll give me a few minutes," I said. "Until then, the Sloane Monroe shop of questions and answers is closed."

We squared off while he thought about how much he wanted to press a friend of the senator, and then the shorter one jabbed the taller one in the side and said, "Let's grab a cup of coffee, Pearce."

The taller one glared at me. "Stay put."

And then both officers walked away.

I grabbed a few tissues off a nearby counter, and Victoria and I sat down.

"Have you seen him yet?" she asked. "Is he awake?"

I shook my head. "Noel's with him now. I'm sure James will be glad you're here."

She dabbed her eyes with the tissue and took a deep breath.

"We need to find this guy," she said. "If we don't, he'll just keep on killing, and if anything else happens to James … I … I just …"

"We'll find him," I said.

"But no one has any idea who he is."

"You're right, but there's something different about this killer than the ones I've tracked in the past. I'm hoping that gives me an edge I haven't had before."

"What kind of edge?"

"The killer had the chance to end my life tonight, and he didn't do it. I don't know what it means yet, but it means something."

"Are you serious? What happened?"

I told her.

Her take was different than mine.

"Maybe he was going to kill you after he jammed the paper inside your shoe," she said, "but he didn't get the chance. All I know is he's murdered three people in less than a month. James was his intended fourth, and something tells me he's not done yet."

Noel walked up, looked at me, and said, "James is still fairly drugged up, but he's awake, if you want to visit with him for a minute. No heavy conversation, but he's asking about you. I'm sure he'd like to see for himself that you're all right."

I nodded. "Would it be okay for Victoria to say hello first?"

Noel shrugged. "I don't see why not. We just need to keep the visits brief."

I agreed, and we walked to his room.

"I don't know what to say," she said. "And I'm a mess. I don't want him to see me like this. You should go in, Sloane. I'll see him later."

"He'd want to know you're here. Besides, I think it will be good for him to see you like this."

"Are you kidding? I'm a disaster."

"The other day when you were talking to me about James. You don't just regret what happened, you still love him, don't you?"

She glanced down the hall, avoiding eye contact with me.

"Victoria," I said, "do you know what I think James would appreciate after all the hell he's been through tonight?"

"I don't know. What?"

"He'd like to know you feel for him the same way he still feels about you."

CHAPTER 22

I left the hospital with Noel, and we drove to my hotel. I packed my things, checked out, and relocated to James' guesthouse. Grace was with Sonia, Noel's other daughter, and given we'd left the hospital in the middle of the night he had decided to let her sleep over and pick her up the following morning.

I spent part of the night soaking in a jetted tub about double the size of the one at the hotel, trying to get into the mindset of the killer. I believed his first two murders were premeditated, but what had happened with Adelaide and James seemed a lot more spontaneous. His knowledge of Shakespeare suggested he was well-read, possibly even sophisticated, and someone who most likely fit into the society norm.

Whoever he was or wasn't, there was something about this case that I wasn't seeing. It was as if I was trying to construct a home with a blindfold on. There was still too much I was missing.

The next morning, Noel left the house, returning around an hour later with Grace. I got ready and set my agenda for the day, starting with a trip to Caroline's office. On the way to the car, I spotted Grace lounging on a hammock on the back porch. She waved at me. I waved back and walked over to her.

"I was hoping I'd see you while I was here," I said.

She stared at me for a while and then said, "I remember you."

"We met the week of your uncle's wedding."

She scrunched up her nose like she'd smelled something rotten. "I'm glad he didn't marry that woman. I didn't like her."

I sat on the porch beside her. "How have you been doing?"

"I'm sad every day."

"I'm sorry. You will start to feel better, but it will take some time."

"That's what everyone says, but no one knows what it feels like to be me."

"You're right."

"Thank you for getting my clothes."

"Is there anything I can do for you while I'm here?" I asked.

She thought about it. "What about a cheeseburger?"

"You want a cheeseburger right now? For breakfast?"

She nodded. "Cheeseburgers are good any time of the day. They're comfort food, you know."

"I can pick one up for you."

"When?"

"As soon as I leave."

She looked at me like she wondered why a fire hadn't been lit under my ass so I could leave right now.

"Where do you want your cheeseburger from?" I asked.

"Happy Burger. You're going to get it and come back, right? I'm hungry."

I nodded.

"Good," she said. "You should have one with me. And you better get one for Grandpa. He's always hungry, and he doesn't like the food Uncle James' cook makes. He says it's far too sophisticated."

We both laughed.

She pulled part of her T-shirt over her face like a protective covering, and I wondered if she was nervous. Through the fabric, she said, "I'm glad he's dead."

The comment caught me off-guard. "You're glad *who's* dead?"

"Nobody. Never mind. It doesn't matter."

"Do you mean Hugh, your mother's boyfriend?"

"Yeah, maybe. You say 'mother,' and I say 'mum.' That's funny."

She glanced across the yard at a yellow butterfly that had just landed on the fence post. I got the impression she wanted to say more about Hugh, and I wasn't sure whether she didn't because she wanted me to go get the burgers or because she thought she shouldn't.

"I never met your mother," I said. "Or Hugh."

"You would have liked her. She was nice. You wouldn't have liked him, though. He was a bad person."

"What didn't you like about him? Was he mean to you?"

She shrugged. "He was fine to me, but he was mean to my mum sometimes."

I thought about how adamant James had been about me not talking to Grace. He'd painted a picture of a girl who was too fragile to talk about anything yet. But sitting here now, she didn't seem as delicate as he'd made her out to be. Even though she was suffering, she was a lot stronger than he gave her credit for, and I was torn. I wanted to respect his wishes, but I was desperate for answers I hoped she could provide, and there was no way of knowing whether or not I'd get the opportunity again.

I decided to press on.

"What did Hugh do to your mother that you thought was mean?"

She shrugged. "It doesn't matter. He's dead now. She's in heaven, and he's where horrible people go when they die. I had a mean cat once. Her name was Cass, but I called her Ass even though my mum didn't like it because it was a swear word, but I didn't care. That's what she was—a big, supersized ass. She died a few years ago, and I bet she's at the bad place with Hugh, and they're sitting on a dark storm cloud somewhere being gigantic asses together."

She'd spoken plainly, with a straight face, and although it shouldn't have been funny, it was, and I had to stop myself from laughing.

"Maybe you're right," I said. "Maybe they are together."

She squinted at me.

"Are you going to get me that cheeseburger, or what?" she said. "Remember when I said I was hungry, like two minutes ago? I'm even hungrier now."

I had hoped to keep her distracted just long enough to get a little more information. I thought about the bruising found on Caroline's body during the autopsy. What I didn't know was whether Grace was aware of it or not.

"I'll go in a minute," I said. "I promise. Can I show you something first?"

She rolled her eyes. "I guess so, but only if you hurry."

I lifted my shirt up just high enough for her to see a two-inch scar I had on my side. It wasn't the only scar I had on my body. But for demonstration purposes, it would suffice.

She leaned forward and pressed two fingers against the wound. "Wow. That's so funny looking. It's shaped like a kangaroo ear. Does it hurt?"

"It did at first. But it happened many years ago. I don't feel any pain now."

"What happened?"

"My father wasn't a good person," I said. "When my sister and I were young, and he was drunk, sometimes he'd come after us with his belt."

"And he would hit you with it?"

I nodded.

"Why?" she asked.

"No reason, really. He had a bad temper. He had a belt buckle he liked to wear that had a skull with wings in the center. The wings stuck out, and they were thin and sharp. One time when he swung the belt at me, the wings broke my skin. My dad yanked the belt back, and the wings tore some of my skin off. I was bleeding, but he wouldn't let my mother take me to the hospital to get it stitched up. She tried to do it herself, and it got infected. That's why I have that nasty scar."

She locked eyes with me, and I could tell she was struggling to keep from crying. I reached out and grabbed her hand.

"I'm sorry, Grace," I said. "I didn't mean to upset you."

"You didn't. I'm fine. Your dad is a bad man … a very bad man. Is he still alive?"

I shook my head.

"And are you sad he's dead?" she asked.

"I'm glad he's dead because he can't hurt anyone ever again."

She rubbed her hands up and down her dress. "I wanted to protect my mum, and I couldn't."

Finally, I was getting somewhere.

"Protect her from Hugh or someone else?"

In what I considered to be the worst possible timing, the front door opened, and Noel walked outside. "I've made poached eggs on toast. You two care for some breakfast?"

Grace glanced at him and burst into tears. She hopped off the hammock, pressed her hands to her face, and ran past him into the house, yelling, "I just want a cheeseburger!"

He watched her scurry down the hall and then turned toward me. "Well, what's going on with her? She usually likes it when I make breakfast."

"We were talking about my father who passed away," I said, "and she got really upset. I'm sorry. I didn't think it would upset her, but I was wrong. I shouldn't have said anything."

He placed a hand on my shoulder. "Don't feel bad. She has good days, and she has bad ones. It looks like today will probably be a bad one. She's confused, you see, all bottled up, and she won't talk to anyone about it. I saw you out here a few minutes ago and thought talking to you might do her some good. Maybe I was wrong too. Maybe neither of us knows what she needs."

"James asked me not to talk to her yet," I said. "He thinks she needs more time. He's probably right."

"I know what he wants. He told me. He's trying to keep her away from just about everyone. I don't agree with it. Not talking about what she went through is keeping her from the chance to heal. We can't go on pretending like nothing happened forever. It did happen, and we all need to accept it—most of all, Grace."

I stood. "I'll run to the burger place and get her a cheeseburger."

"One word of advice if I may before you head out," he said.

I nodded, expecting his next words to be profound and encouraging.

Instead, he winked at me and said, "If you don't want her to complain, better make sure her burger has extra cheese."

CHAPTER 23

I dropped the cheeseburgers off to Noel and decided to give Grace some space before approaching her again. In turn, Noel handed me a note Grace had written to me. He said she had been in her room since I left and had only cracked her door open to pass the note to him. It said: *Thank you for the cheeseburger. I want to stay in my room today and watch movies. See you later. P.S. I'm sorry about your dad, but don't worry. He's in the bad place with Hugh and Ass-cat.*

James was doing better today, but he wouldn't be released from the hospital yet. Officer Pearce had been stationed outside his room, and an additional two officers continued to keep watch on James' house. The chief superintendent assured Noel that what happened before wouldn't happen again, but it was a promise he shouldn't have made. The killer was still out there ... and unpredictable. No one knew his next move.

Noel followed me out to my car. As I got in, he handed me a small, black tote bag.

"What's this?" I asked.

"Look inside," he said. "But don't take it out. Not right now."

I pulled the bag open, staring down at the gun at the bottom of the bag.

"It just doesn't feel right to let you go out without it," he said. "Just keep it out of sight, okay? And don't get caught with it."

I'd always carried a gun in the past, but the laws here were different, making me hesitant to accept his offering. I did anyway.

"I respect Australia's gun laws," he said. "They're in place for a good reason. But this is a unique situation. We're being hunted by a savage animal, and I'm not about to let you go straight at him empty-handed."

I thanked him and backed out of the driveway.

I switched the radio on. The host was going over the top news headlines of the day, surprising me when she said a representative speaking on James' behalf had formally announced he was resigning from his senate position in order to deal with personal issues at home.

I'd planned on heading to Caroline's office, but Grace's emotional outburst had me rattled and wondering why she'd been triggered by what I'd said. Maybe she knew her mother had been physically abused. There was one person I hoped could provide answers to my questions—the boy she'd been dating, Tommy Walker.

Tommy lived in an upscale suburb of Cairns called City View. I parked curbside, placed the bag Noel had given me in the glove box, and got out of the car, taking a moment to admire the surrounding area from his parents' residence, which was situated high enough above the city to offer a spectacular, sweeping view of Cairns. I leaned against my car, breathing it in, and my thoughts turned to Cade. When last we spoke on the phone the night before he was finalizing the sale of his home in Jackson Hole. When I returned home, we would be free spirits with the ability to go anywhere. I couldn't wait to discuss where we would put roots down next.

A brown-haired, blue-eyed boy approached the car, standing in front of me with his legs spread and his arms crossed. He gave me a look that indicated strangers weren't welcome on his property, and then he started in on a series of questions.

"Who are you?" he asked. "Why are you parked in front of my house?"

"Are you Tommy Walker?" I asked.

"I am. You didn't answer my questions."

"You know Grace, right? Grace Ashby?"

"Yeah, how do *you* know her?"

"My name is Sloane Monroe. I'm friends with James, her uncle."

The boy took a step back, providing a bit more space between him and my personal bubble, which he'd just penetrated.

He relaxed his shoulders. "I've been calling the senator for days. What's the deal with him, anyway? Is he okay? My mum said he was attacked in the park last night."

I nodded. "He had surgery last night, and it went well. He's expected to recover."

I considered whether or not I should have been giving him any information at all. For all I knew, the kid was the killer. But everything I'd said so far had already been vocalized on the news for public consumption. It wasn't a secret. And as far as appearances went, Tommy didn't look like a killer. Then again, killers didn't always look like killers. Nurse and soccer mom Kristen Gilbert was about as innocent-looking as one could be, and she'd injected her patients with adrenaline.

"How's Grace doing?" he asked. "Have you seen her? Is she all right?"

"She's fine. I was with her this morning."

"And?"

"She's doing about how you'd expect for someone who just lost her mother."

"Did she ask you to come here?"

"No."

"Then I'll ask again ... why are you here?"

"You never asked why I was here. You asked why I was parked in front of your house. See the difference?"

Based on the look on his face, I considered dialing down the sarcasm.

"Grace got upset this morning," I said, "and I thought you might know why."

"How would I know? I don't know how she's doing because her stupid uncle won't let me see her."

"He's not really letting her see anyone right now," I said.

"He let her see *you*."

It wasn't true, but he didn't need to know that.

"What did you think of Hugh, her mother's boyfriend?" I asked.

"I didn't like the guy."

"Why not?"

He shrugged. "Lots of reasons."

"Such as?"

"Why do you want to know?"

"Do you know what Grace's relationship was like with Hugh and what it was like with her mother?"

He tilted his head and stared at me. "Your accent sounds funny. Where are you from? Canada?"

"I'm from America."

"You have a wacky president. He sends funny tweets on Twitter."

I smiled. "From what I hear, *you* have a wacky prime minister."

"If you're not from here, then how do you know Grace's uncle?"

I told him about my previous visit to Australia.

"You don't really know him, though," he said. "Why are you back in Cairns?"

Bright kid.

"James invited me here. I'm trying to find the person responsible for the murders of Caroline, Hugh, and Adelaide, and for the attempted murder of James."

"Is that what you do—you hunt killers?"

I nodded. Close enough.

"Do you know who he is?" he asked. "Have you found him?"

Maybe I had. Maybe I was standing in front of him now.

"I haven't yet," I said. "But I will. When was the last time you saw Grace?"

He wagged a finger in front of me. "Not fair. Trick question."

"It isn't a trick question. I heard Caroline got upset about your relationship with Grace and told you not to come over for a while. Did that upset you?"

"I love Grace ... so yeah. Her mum shouldn't have tried to keep us apart. She can't keep us apart. No one can."

"What does that mean?"

He shook his head. "You think I'm a suspect, huh? That's why you're here."

"At the moment, everyone is."

"Well, I'm not. I didn't do *anything* to her mum. I'd never do anything to hurt Grace."

"You had a problem with her keeping the two of you apart, though, right?"

"Not really. I knew it wouldn't last."

"Do you know anyone who didn't like Caroline or Hugh, or how their murders could be connected to Adelaide and the attack on James?"

He thought about it. "What if someone is murdering people James cares about to get back at him for something he did?"

"Like what?" I asked.

"Did you see the news today?"

"I heard it."

"I was thinking ... what if maybe this guy was trying to get the senator to quit all along?"

And now he had.

"Why would anyone go to such extreme lengths? And what reason would someone have to go after his family?"

He narrowed his eyes, looking at me like I was naïve. "Politicians are idiots. They're all stupid. Even my dad says so."

"Let's say there's truth to your theory. It would explain Caroline's murder, but not the other two."

He shrugged. "How would I know?"

"What do you think of James?"

"He won't let me see Grace."

"Did he say why?"

"*He* didn't say anything. His office lady told me."

"Maybe I can talk to him and see if I can get him to change his mind."

He raised a brow. "Why? You don't know me."

"I don't, but Grace does, and I think she needs you in her life right now."

It wasn't something I planned on doing, not until I ruled him out as a suspect. I'd said it to elicit favor, and given the fact he'd just cracked a smile, the idea had worked.

"Sure," he said, "if you think it would help."

"I imagine it's been hard not seeing her all this time."

He laughed. "Yeah, well, it hasn't been as long as you think."

"What do you mean?"

"I broke the rules. We just wanted to be together."

"How many times have you seen Grace since Caroline asked you to stay away?"

He rubbed his hands together. "I ... I don't know if I should say. Never mind."

I was losing him.

"You know, I did the same thing once when I was your age. My mother didn't like the guy I'd been seeing, and she forbade me to see him again."

"What did you do?"

"I opened my bedroom window and piled a stack of clothes in front of it. After my mom went to bed, I waited until the heater kicked on, and then I snuck out."

"Did you ever get caught?"

I nodded. "One night we were out driving around and my mother's best friend saw me in the car with my boyfriend. I went home, expecting my mom to ground me for life. The weird thing was … she didn't. She changed tactics and started inviting my boyfriend to the house. It didn't take long for me to realize I didn't like him as much as I thought I did, and we broke up."

"I'd never break up with Grace. I love her."

"I believe you, and I believe she loves you. How many times have you seen her?"

"Every night. Well, every night until her mum died and she moved in with her uncle. He has more security cameras. I'm scared he'd catch me."

He. Saw. Her. Every. Night.

Every night *without* getting caught.

"How did you do it?" I asked.

"Caroline went to bed at eleven and woke up at six. I waited until the lights were out, and then I went to Grace's bedroom window and tapped three times. She'd let me in, and I'd sleep next to her all night. Then I'd sneak back out and go home."

An obvious, burning question came to mind. "Were you at Grace's house the night of the murder? Did you see what happened?"

He stared at the ground. "I don't want to talk about it."

Not talking about it *was* talking about it. He *hadn't* said no.

"Please, Tommy," I said. "I'm only trying to help the family get closure so they can move on. Just tell me what happened. If you do, I can protect Grace. I know you know something. Help me help her."

He pounded his fist onto his chest. "*I* protect Grace. I'm the only one. Not her mum, not her uncle, not her grandfather, and not you. *Me.* The only reason you're really here is to get me to tell you things."

"And what should you be telling me?"

"Nothing. *He* can tell you if he wants. I'm not doing it."

"He … who?"

"I can't talk to you anymore."

"Of course you can," I said.

"No, I can't. You tell the senator I love Grace. You tell him I don't care if he lets her see me or not. No one can keep her away from me."

CHAPTER 24

The man was agitated.

He had spared the foreigner's life, giving her a single reprieve when he could have chosen to end her, and still, she was nosing around like an ungrateful little bitch.

Why couldn't she leave things alone?

He knew now that he'd been remiss in sparing her life, in giving her an opportunity to leave the country, removing herself from the unfortunate situation she had found herself in. He was sure she'd find the note he left, realize how close she'd come to death, and be too afraid to remain any longer.

He'd been wrong.

So wrong.

To infect his wounded ego even further, as it turned out, the senator *wasn't* dead either (an egregious oversight on the man's part), and now the foreigner was running amuck, sprinkling herself in places she didn't belong.

The foreigner was getting a lot closer to the truth than the man was comfortable with, and when the morning news revealed her as a friend of the family, they'd given her name. The man had written it down, surprised when he did an internet search and found out her true identity.

She wasn't there for the senator, as once the man presumed.

She wasn't just a friend of his either, visiting to show support after the loss of his sister.

She was there for *him*, to hunt him down.

And she wasn't leaving until she *had* him.

He would go after her again—only this time, he'd show no mercy.

CHAPTER 25

After Tommy proclaimed no one could keep him from Grace, he'd abruptly whipped around and sprinted back to his house. I chased after him, asking for a chance to fix whatever I had broken between us. He wasn't interested, and when the door slammed in my face right before I reached it, I stood there for a moment, trying to decide what to do next.

Then I started knocking.

Tommy's mother answered, a five-foot-nothing petite woman with brunette hair braided into a loose bun, wearing a bright, floral sundress and flip-flops. With one hand on her hip, she scolded me over her son being so upset. I tried to explain, and she interrupted me, saying she didn't care what had been said between us. Her son had been through enough. She didn't like seeing him agitated for any reason. I was strongly advised never to return to their house again, following which she shut the door in the same manner Tommy had done a minute earlier.

Even though I'd pinched a nerve, and Tommy had become defensive over Grace, our conversation was a productive one. I sat in my car, going over what he had said, and I attempted to fill in the blanks of what he hadn't. His words played over and over in my mind, like a message I had the ability to decode if I considered it long enough.

I thought about the quote found inside my shoe.

Then the liars and swearers are fools, for there are liars and swearers enough to beat the honest men and hang up them.

Adelaide was the liar.

James was the fool.

A fool, by definition, was a person tricked or deceived into appearing or acting silly or stupid, thus making him a liar himself.

Maybe there was something to Tommy's suggestion that the murders were politically motivated and had something to do with James. But as far as I knew, Adelaide had no hand in James' political dealings. If Adelaide and James were *both* "swearers," as the quote suggested, there was a connection between them, one I was certain I didn't understand yet.

CHAPTER 26

James was sitting up in his hospital bed, watching the news, and sipping on a cup of coffee when I walked in.

"Good to see you, Sloane," he said. "Did you get my text?"

I nodded. "Did you get mine?"

"You said we needed to talk. I was thinking the same thing."

I pulled a chair closer to his bed and sat down. "I know you've been through a lot lately. You've just lost your sister, and you're grieving. You've also assumed custody of Grace and have been trying to help her recover. And you're looking out for your dad too. It's a lot to deal with, a lot of pressure, but I don't think it's the only pressure you've been under."

"You're right. That's why I've decided to step down as senator. I can't focus on the job *and* my family *and* a murderer who hasn't been caught yet and maintain my position and perform the duties expected of me. It's not what I want, but it's what needs to happen."

"I get it," I said, "but the added pressure of your job isn't what I was talking about."

He raised a brow. "It's not? What are you trying to say, then?"

"I've been sitting in my car in the hospital parking lot for the last hour, thinking about you and Adelaide and why you were both targeted by the killer. It seems odd to me that you two were labeled as a liar and a fool, and yet the killer didn't send any kind of message when he killed Caroline and Hugh."

"I'm not sure what to tell you. Who knows what the reasons are for what he's doing? It takes a certain kind of person to kill another person. You have to understand, we could be dealing with someone who isn't in his right mind."

I understood just fine.

"In the park, he could have easily gotten rid of me if he'd wanted to," I said, "and he didn't. Why do you think that is?"

"When we catch him, we'll ask him, and then you'll have your answer."

His comment had been peppered with a hint of sarcasm, and I was just getting started.

"Is there anything you need to tell me?" I asked. "Anything you should have told me before now but didn't?"

He set the coffee cup down and crossed his arms. "I'm not sure what you're looking for me to say here, Sloane. I get the feeling you've come here today to play guessing games with me, and I'm in no mood for it. I thought we were headed in the right direction together. Was I wrong?"

"I went to see Tommy Walker today."

He shrugged. "And? What did he have to say?"

"Tommy told me if I wanted to know what happened the night of your sister's murder, the part I *don't* know about, I should ask you."

I was paraphrasing, and it wasn't exactly what Tommy had said, but for now, it was all I had to work with. I hoped it was enough to provoke him to talk.

"What makes Tommy think he knows *anything*?"

"You heard the killer pushed a quote into my shoe, right?" I said.

He nodded. "Yeah, I heard."

"I believe the killer was trying to send me a message."

"Why you? Why not communicate with the paper again if he's so desperate to reach out?"

"He wrote to the paper, and nothing came of it. Maybe he thought he'd try a different avenue this time. Did you know Tommy was still seeing Grace every night, even after Caroline said he couldn't?"

James looked at me like he was shocked at the news, but I wasn't sure I believed it.

"What?" he asked. "How?"

I relayed what Tommy had told me and then added, "He said he was there every night, *including* the night of the murders."

Another partial "truth," which may or may not have been true.

I wondered if he'd buy it.

James closed his eyes and leaned back on the pillow. "Tommy actually said he was there the night of the murders? Did he see something he hasn't told anyone about?"

"I don't know. You were there too. You didn't see him?"

"No, I didn't. You're second-guessing what I've told you. I don't like it."

"No more smoke and mirrors, James. No more misleading me. Whatever you're keeping from me and everyone else … well, I came all this way to help you. I deserve to be given the story in its entirety, and not one with holes in it."

"I gave you the story. Maybe you should take the rest of the day off and cool down."

I leaned forward, looking him in the eye. "How many more people have to die before you trust me? Tommy? Me? Your father? Grace? Victoria?"

"Stop it, Sloane."

I slid my chair back against the wall and stood. "All right, fine. I'll stop. Seems there's nothing more for us to say to each other today. Instead of pressing Tommy for more information, I thought I'd come here and talk to you instead. Until now, you've always seemed like a stand-up guy, a man others respect. But you obviously don't trust me, and you should. I've been on your side this entire time, and I almost got myself killed trying to protect you. But, hey, no big deal."

I slung my bag over my shoulder, walked to the door, and threw it open.

"Just ... hang on, Sloane. Wait a minute."

"No. I'm done hanging on to half-truths and missing facts."

"I *do* trust you. I wouldn't have brought you here if I didn't see the same qualities in you that I see in myself."

I stood in the doorway, desperate to walk out, but telling myself I'd be an idiot to do so when it seemed he was on the brink of enlightening me.

"Yeah, well, there's no use in me trying to solve these murders if I'm missing an important piece to the puzzle," I said.

"I never wanted to keep anything from you. It's complicated, more complicated than you know."

"I realized how complicated it must be just this morning when I thought about the kind of person you are. You place a great deal of value on the truth. Hell, you canceled your wedding last year after finding out your fiancée lied to you. Whatever it is, I know it's heavy. But I'm not leaving this place until the murders are solved, and if that means uncovering whatever you're keeping from me and everyone else in the process, so be it."

"You don't want to do that."

"Actually, I do."

Actually, I didn't. All I really wanted was for him to level with me.

"Trust me, you don't," he said. "Some burdens are best borne alone. It's better off this way. You can solve the case without it."

I glanced back at him. "What am I missing that's so bad, James? How awful could it be?"

"Would it help if I told you I'd behave the same way if I were in your position?"

"It wouldn't."

He sighed. "Everything I'm doing, all of it has been about protecting Grace."

CHAPTER 27

James and I stared at one another like two friends engaged in a standoff neither of us wanted to have. Gazing into his eyes, I saw many things—pain, fear, and a pleading desperation I never thought I'd see in a man so refined and sophisticated. Flashes of everything I'd heard and experienced since the plane touched down rushed through my head like explosives detonating at the same time:

The killer's quotes.

The labels the killer had given to Adelaide and James.

James keeping me away from Grace.

Grace yanking her shirt over her face when we'd talked.

Tommy saying he'd do *anything* for her.

James acting out of desperation.

The root of all I wanted to know was in figuring out why James was so desperate. He wasn't just protecting Grace from the killer. He was protecting her from something else. When it hit me and the moment of clarity came, I realized James had been right.

Some burdens *were* best borne alone.

CHAPTER 28

The moment of full transparency came like a sledgehammer to the face. When Grace had pulled her shirt over her face earlier that morning, I had been so caught up in assuming she was uncomfortable by my presence, what we were discussing, and my concern over what I could do to keep her talking that I'd grossly misinterpreted her actions. She may have used her shirt as a safety blanket, but that wasn't the *only* reason she'd covered up.

James looked at me as if he was aware I had connected the dots and was waiting for me to start talking again to confirm it.

"You told me Grace found Hugh hovering over her mother and that she escaped out of the bathroom window and ran to Adelaide's house, where she called you," I said. "It's not true, though, is it? That's not the order of events exactly the way they happened."

He took a deep breath and pointed across the room. "If we're going to have this conversation, you'd better close the door."

I did.

"Maybe it was wrong for me to bring you into the situation and think I could keep you in the dark," he said. "I've thought about talking to you about it a few times."

"Why didn't you?"

"I thought I was looking out for everyone's interests—Grace's, my family's, and yours."

I believed him.

I walked over to the table, poured myself a glass of water, and downed the entire thing.

"I saw Grace this morning," I said. "And you know something? When the sun hit her T-shirt just right, it became a little see-through, and I could have sworn I saw a dark patch on her skin, right below her left shoulder. It was a flash, no more than a moment, and I decided it was nothing more than a shadow reflecting off the sun because of how she was sitting. Now I know I was wrong. I did see something. She has bruises on her body, doesn't she?"

He nodded.

"James," I said, "what *really* happened that night?"

CHAPTER 29

It was Grace who had murdered Hugh, *not* the killer.

I didn't want to believe it, even when it came straight from James' mouth, but I had to, because it was true.

"After finding Caroline dead and Hugh hovering over her like he was to blame, Grace and Hugh had argued," James said. "She ran to the bathroom and locked herself inside, planning to escape out of the window and run to Adelaide's house."

That much I knew.

"Grace was angry," he said. "And you have to understand, she thinks differently than we do. In her mind, Hugh killed Caroline, and she was sure of it. Instead of going out the window, she ran back into the bedroom, grabbed the knife, and started swinging."

"Hugh fought back, and at some point, she cut his neck. What happened next?"

"Hugh ran out of the room. She chased him. When they got to the banister at the top of the stairs, he turned around, trying to reason with her. She kept on swinging. He started down the stairs but lost his footing and fell to his death."

Things were clearer now and yet still hazy at the same time. "You brought me here to find Caroline's killer. If Hugh *had* done it, you wouldn't have asked for my help. How do you *know* Hugh didn't kill Caroline?"

"I installed security cameras at the front and back of Caroline's property last year. When Hugh walked up to the door that night, inside the house you can hear Caroline screaming for her life and Hugh desperately trying to get the door open to get to her."

"Why didn't you give the video footage to the police?"

"Grace is on it. There's a clear video of her running out of the house with blood on her clothes, carrying the knife. What happened to Hugh was bad enough. I didn't want the police assuming she'd killed Caroline, too."

"Why couldn't she have explained what happened? He fell. It was an accident."

"*You* see it that way, and *I* see it that way, but there's no way to be sure how it would have been seen by the police. Hugh fell because he was trying to get away from Grace, which makes her somewhat responsible for his death."

Hearing the story now, I understood his need to protect her and his reasons for doing it.

"Where is the surveillance video now?"

"I have it, and I am the only one who has watched it."

"Didn't the police find it strange that the footage was gone?"

He shook his head. "I told them the cameras had been broken for months."

And they'd believed him because they had no reason not to.

"Is there any footage of the killer entering or exiting the house on the video?"

He shook his head. "I've watched it over and over. He didn't enter through the front or back door. I assume he found a blind spot and went through a window."

"What about the bruises found on Caroline's body?" I asked. "When I asked you before you acted as though you didn't know where they came from. What about now?"

"Hugh and Caroline got into a fight recently. He threw her up against the wall and used his arm to try to pin her there so she couldn't move. She shoved him, trying to get free, and he threw her to the ground. Grace saw it happen and tackled him. He pushed her off of him, bruising her shoulder in the process."

"Why did you keep this from me?"

"I figured if you knew Hugh was responsible for the bruises, you'd assume Hugh had killed Caroline and then fell down the stairs somehow to his death. I wanted to be sure you were invested in finding the real killer."

"How do you know about the fight between Caroline and Hugh? Did Caroline tell you?"

"Grace told me a few weeks ago. Caroline kicked Hugh out after the incident. He left the next morning for a work conference in Sydney, and Caroline told Grace as soon as he returned, she planned on breaking up with him."

Grace saw Hugh kneeling over Caroline's body and assumed he'd killed her mother because her mother told him she wanted the relationship to be over. I thought about what Tommy had said about sneaking through Grace's window at night. It made sense that he might have dealt with his frustration over not seeing Grace by killing Caroline to get her out of the way, especially after he'd just insisted no one would keep them apart. It was also possible Hugh either caught Tommy in the act or Tommy heard Hugh arrive and hid from view. The theories were plausible, and the best I'd come up with so far. If true, there was one gaping hole: Tommy still didn't have what he wanted.

CHAPTER 30

The enlightenment recently bestowed upon me by James had come at a price, one in which I would need to make a decision. Did I keep Grace's secret as he had done, or did I hold her responsible for her actions even though Hugh's death was a gray area, one that I was currently trying to reconcile within myself? Hugh had abused her mother, but did that mean he deserved to die for it? Grace's only objective that night was to avenge her mother. Did that mean she deserved to be put on trial, which could lead to a possible murder sentence?

I couldn't decide, which was a decision in itself. Until I was sure I knew everything that had happened the night the murders began, I would keep the matter to myself.

"Who else knows about what Grace did?" I asked.

"Adelaide knew, of course," James said.

"What about Tommy?"

"I was telling you the truth earlier. If he was at the house that night, I know nothing of it."

"What about your dad and Victoria? What do they know?"

"Victoria suspects *something*. I can tell by the questions she asked me after she performed the autopsies. But so far, I haven't revealed anything to her."

"Why not?"

"I don't want to put her in the same position I just put you. Besides, the more people who know, the harder it is to contain."

"Did Adelaide agree you should keep it to yourselves?"

He nodded. "She was certain it was in Grace's best interest. Up to the day Adelaide died, I thought I'd made the right choice. Now, I'm not sure. The killer has made it clear he's coming after us because we lied, because we've tried to pin both murders on him. Personally, I don't understand. He committed murder either way. Why does he care whether he gets the blame for an additional one he didn't commit? When he's caught, it won't make much of a difference, especially now that he has added to the numbers."

But the killer did care. He cared a lot.

"Your dad was in law enforcement for a long time," I said. "I'm surprised he didn't notice something wasn't right."

"He's been too busy grieving and watching out for us to focus on the gaps in the story. Tracking a killer is a lot different when the connection is personal. It muddies things and affects a person's judgment. He isn't himself."

None of them were.

"I understand why you didn't tell me," I said. "I still don't like it, but I get it."

"And now I am at your mercy. We both are. What will you do now?"

"Nothing," I said. "I need time to figure everything out. Your focus should be on how this is all affecting Grace. She's a mess, James. I'm guessing she feels like she can't talk about it because you and Adelaide probably told her not to discuss it with anyone."

"We did. We had to. It's for her own good."

"Is it, though? I'm not sure she can live with the lie. Does she even know Hugh didn't kill her mother?"

He nodded. "Not through me. Adelaide was talking to her after Caroline's funeral and let it slip. Adelaide stupidly thought I'd told Grace, but why would I? It would have been better for her to go through life thinking what she did was justified. Now she'll go through it feeling even guiltier about it."

She'd also go through life trying to convince herself Hugh was a bad person, like she was doing now.

"I don't want to see her punished any more than you do," I said, "but is what you're doing really the lesser of two evils? She'll punish herself forever for what she did, whether she takes accountability for it or not."

"You're right, but nothing can undo what's been done. Why put her through all the public scrutiny? She's not a murderer. She's not a bad person. She's a good girl who made an honest mistake."

"The killer knows about the 'honest mistake,' though. Aren't you concerned he'll come for her next?"

"We don't know what he knows. All he's sure of is that he didn't kill Hugh."

"I know you're trying to protect her," I said. "I just don't think the way you're going about it is for the best."

"If it would make you feel better to remove yourself from this situation, I understand. You can go home, and I'll take it from here."

It felt like I'd just been slugged in the face, like all I'd done so far had been worth nothing. "Don't talk down to me just because I'm giving you advice you don't want to hear. I'm invested in this case."

"You've done plenty for my family already. If you stay, you're putting yourself in even more danger. When I asked you to come here, I didn't know more murders would follow."

"I wouldn't feel right about leaving. It isn't an option, so stop talking to me like it is."

"If it's about the money—"

"It isn't."

He threw his hands in the air.

"All right. I understand. What's your next step, and what can I do to help?"

"I need to speak to Tommy again. I want to find out what else he knows and confirm whether he had something to do with Caroline's death."

"I want to believe he wasn't responsible. If we can confirm it, maybe I should allow Grace to see him. Maybe it would help. She asks to call him every day, and I always say no, thinking that keeping her in the house and away from everyone is in her best interest. But without anything to distract her, I can see now how that's a problem."

"She's lucky to have you in her life. You've done a good job trying to keep your family together through this. Any idea how long you'll be in the hospital?"

"Until tomorrow, at least."

"Now that everything is out in the open, will you tell your father?" I asked.

"I will, but it needs to be in my own way, when the time is right."

James' cell phone rang, signaling the perfect time for me to make my exit, but as soon as the person on the other end of the line began talking, James' facial expression soured. I was curious, so I stayed.

When the call ended, I said, "What's wrong?"

"You'll need to hold off on visiting Tommy Walker again."

"Why? What's happened?"

James ran a hand across his face. "I've just spoken to the police. Tommy's mum called a few minutes ago. He's missing."

CHAPTER 31

The man popped open the trunk of his vintage Chevrolet Corvair, a car his grandfather had left to him ten years ago after he'd been diagnosed with terminal cancer. The man wanted to feel special, like his grandfather had left his precious car to him because of the special bond they shared. The truth was, the man's father hadn't wanted it, and given the man was one of only two grandchildren, the decision wasn't a hard one to make. Once, the man's father had even joked about his dad flipping a coin to decide which of his two grandkids would get the car, but since his grandfather was dead now, it was hard to know whether his father had been telling him the truth or not. Either way, the man appreciated the gesture and had taken superb care of the vintage classic. If his grandfather could see him now, he was sure he would have agreed he'd chosen the right grandkid to inherit it.

The man lifted the trunk's lid and reached a hand inside, and then quickly recoiled before he had the chance to claim his precious cargo. The cargo was restless, like a wild cat, and had started kicking in the man's direction, smashing a foot into his hand like an immature, ungrateful twat.

To teach his cargo a lesson, the man slammed the trunk closed again.

"I'm trying to be reasonable here, kid," the man said. "But if this is how you're going to treat me, I'll leave you in here forever to rot and waste away. Is that what you want?"

The man didn't mean it, of course. He used a special cleaner to keep the upholstery smelling fresh. The stench of a decaying body would ruin it, just like his mum's bag of peaches had when she'd left them in the back seat until they turned to mush. The smell never did come out.

The man hesitated a moment for effect and then said, "What was that? Did you say something?"

"I'm sorry," the kid mumbled. "I won't do it again. Please, let me out."

"That's better. Still, I want to be sure the valuable lesson I'm teaching here today has been learned. I'm a bit ravenous, so I'm going to go make a sandwich. When I finish, I'll come out here and get you, and we'll try again."

As the kid began to cry, the man shook his head and turned, heading toward the house. Why was the kid crying? He'd just told him he'd be back. That was the problem with teenagers today. They were too damn soft.

The man walked into the kitchen, removed a loaf of homemade bread he'd baked recently, and sliced it, pausing a moment to hold one of the pieces under his nose and take a big whiff. It was perfect, just like always.

He buttered the bread, fried it in a pan, and set the slices on a plate. Returning to the pan, he rubbed a spicy sauce mixture over a few barramundi fillets, a variety of delicious Asian sea bass, and grilled it. In the meantime, he whipped up a coleslaw mixture to spread over the sauce. When everything was finished, he took a step back, marveling at yet another spectacular masterpiece. The presentation itself was magnificent. He snapped a photo and uploaded it to his food blog with the caption: Succulent Sandwich Saturday, knowing the photo would be a winner with his 9,033 subscribers.

He pulled a chair out and sat down, and then said, "Petey, lunch is ready."

Petey entered the room, smiling as he gazed at the artistry laid out before him.

The man held up the plate and said, "You better eat up. There's an item in the trunk I'll need your help with in a few minutes."

CHAPTER 32

James advised me not to head back over to Tommy's house to talk to his mother until the police had come and gone. At the moment, they were at Tommy's house, questioning his mother about what happened. I knew this because I'd just done a drive-by to see if they were still there.

Tommy had been missing for less than two hours, a timeline the police wouldn't usually take seriously yet, but given his connection to Grace, they were more interested than usual. As far as what had happened, James had only a few details so far. Tommy's mother had sent him to the corner store for a gallon of milk. The owner of the store saw him come in, get the milk, and check out at the register. He walked out the front door and vanished.

There was some speculation about Tommy walking over to see Grace. Knowing James was in the hospital, Tommy may have felt it was the chance he'd been waiting for, and James' house was only twenty minutes away on foot. All the possible routes were checked. There was no sign of Tommy, and the neighbors whom police had talked to along the way hadn't seen him.

I did some speculating of my own and considered I may have spooked Tommy earlier, and now he was on the run. It was much easier to accept than the possibility Tommy might have been nabbed by the killer—an option I didn't want to be true.

It was starting to feel like we were all being picked off one by one.

To make use of my time, I stopped by Caroline's office, a quaint, modern-looking building downtown, which she had shared with other therapists. I walked into the reception area and was greeted by a floor-to-ceiling fountain with tall tropical plants adorning each end. The room smelled clean and fresh, like rain, and the soft lighting of lamps created a calm, soothing illusion that made me feel like I was out in nature instead of inside a large box.

Across the fountain was a plush sofa big enough to sleep on, and sitting in the center of it was a woman with curly, black, shoulder-length hair who appeared to be in her thirties. She had avoided looking at me since I'd walked in, focusing on the magazine folded open on her lap instead. I stared down the hall at three doors. One had a placard with Caroline's name. I fished out the key James had given me and walked toward it.

I stuck the key in the lock, and someone said, "Excuse me, what are you doing?"

The woman put down the magazine she was holding and curled a finger toward herself, indicating she expected me to walk over to her. I didn't want to, but I did.

"Why are you interested in what I'm doing?" I asked. "Are you a patient waiting for an appointment?"

She pressed a hand to her chest like the implication that she was there for a session had offended her. "I'm *not* a patient. I'm waiting for my husband."

"Oh, is *he* a patient?"

She frowned. "No, he isn't. You didn't answer my question."

"And you didn't answer mine," I said.

"How do you know Caroline?"

"I work for her brother, James."

She crossed her legs and leaned back on the sofa, tapping a manicured finger on the magazine.

She pointed at my hand and said, "Oh, I guess that explains why you have a key to Caroline's office, then."

I nodded. "Did you know Caroline well?"

"I did. We were good friends. It's difficult … what happened … on all of us. She was a good person. She didn't deserve to die. What do you do for James?"

"Whatever he needs."

She looked perplexed but didn't head down that road any further.

"How's Grace doing?" she asked. "I've been meaning to stop by and see her."

"She's all right. Do you know of anyone who would have wanted to harm Caroline?"

She raised a brow. "Why are you asking?"

"Until the police solve the case, Caroline's family won't be able to move on. I thought since you two were friends, she might have said something to you."

"Anything I know I've told the police, but to answer your question, no. Caroline was well-liked around here. She was a real sweetheart, and I don't say that about many people."

I believed it.

"Well, someone had it out for her," I said.

"How do you know they had it out for *her*? Maybe they had it out for Hugh. He was a real jerk."

She'd gone prickly again, and I didn't have it in me to keep the banter going any longer. Fortunately, I was saved when one of the other office doors down the hall opened. Two men walked out. One had a perfectly shaved head and wore a navy button-up shirt and boat shorts. The other was Charlie Branson.

CHAPTER 33

The two men walked down the hall. The bald one draped his arm around the prickly woman's shoulder and gave her a squeeze. Charlie walked out the front door without even acknowledging me. I followed him outside.

"Hey, how's it going?" I asked.

He glanced back at me. "Do I know you?"

I wasn't the best when it came to facial recognition, but it seemed odd that he didn't remember me. Today his hair was different. It was the same color but neatly trimmed and short. He reminded me of Edward Norton.

"You cut your hair," I said.

"No, I didn't."

"Yes, you did. You had it in a ponytail when I saw you last."

He threw his hands in the air. "What are you talking about?"

I was starting to feel like I was going crazy. Perhaps I was.

"You're James' lawyer," I said. "We met at the police station. You sat with me when I was being questioned."

He nodded. "Ohh ... I see what's happening here. You're thinking of my cousin, Charlie."

I stared at him for a moment, scanning him up and down before realizing my mistake. The longer I looked at his face, the more I noticed the subtle differences between them.

"I can't believe how much you look alike," I said.

"Yeah, same height, same hairstyle until recently, and we're only one year apart I get it. It happens sometimes."

"Sorry for the mistake."

He stuck his hand out. "I'm Brad."

We shook. "I'm Sloane. I wouldn't have aggressively pursued you if I had known you were someone else. What are you doing here?"

"Martin and I are on a rugby team together. We were just discussing the team dinner after the final game next week."

I assumed Martin was the bald therapist who also worked in Caroline's office.

"There's one other therapist who works here too, right?"

He pointed at himself. "Yeah, me. What are you doing here?"

I wasn't sure if *here* meant Australia or if he was asking why I was standing in front of him. "I'm just grabbing some things out of Caroline's office."

He folded his arms. "Why?"

It wasn't what he asked, but *how* he asked that interested me. "I'm helping James gather some of her things together. He has a lot going on right now."

"I heard. Why was my cousin with you at the police station?"

"I'm sure you've heard about the woman who just died, right? Adelaide Wiggins."

"Yeah."

"I was with her right before she was murdered," I said. "The police just wanted to ask me about it."

"Why were you with her?"

"I was at Caroline's house, picking up some clothes for Grace."

"Another errand for James?"

"Something like that."

"Hey, I think the news said a woman named Sloane was with James when he was attacked at the park. That you too?"

I nodded.

"Seems like you keep finding yourself in the wrong place at the wrong time."

"I could say it's a coincidence," I said.

"You could, but would it be true?"

"What was your relationship like with Caroline?"

He stared at me a moment and then said, "Healthy. Nice meeting you, Sloane."

He walked to his car and got in without saying another word. I tapped on the window. He put it down.

"I wasn't completely honest with you just now," I said. "I mean, I wasn't lying either ... I just wasn't telling you—"

"I know. Care to start again?"

"I'm a private investigator, and I'm here to help solve the recent murders, specifically Caroline's. I've been keeping that part quiet because it could be problematic for me to be here if word gets out about what I'm doing."

I didn't know why I'd just blurted it all out like I had. Maybe because when it came to therapists, I'd always assumed they were trained to know when I was lying, and that had caused me to run my mouth.

"And how's it going—solving her murder?" he asked.

"Not well at the moment. I was hoping I might find something of value in her office."

"Like what?"

"I don't know yet."

"You were honest with me, so I'll be honest with you. I liked her."

"She's like a broken record," I said. "When it comes to her, everyone says the same thing."

"No, I mean, I *liked* her. And I think she liked me too. It's a bit difficult because we were colleagues, but a couple of months ago I took a chance and asked her out."

"Didn't you know she was dating Hugh?"

"I knew she wanted to break it off with him."

"What did she say when you asked her out?"

"She told me she had a lot of things going on and to give her a few months and then ask again. As you know, I never got the chance. She seemed genuinely interested in getting together once things settled down, but I also wondered if she could have already been seeing someone else."

"What makes you think that?"

"She started staying at my place."

"Staying at your place?" I asked.

"Oh, no. Not *with* me. I own a rental house on the ocean. Well, above the ocean. It's close to Fitzroy Island. I had a window installed along the center of the floor. You can sit and watch sea life swim by. It's a great place to stay for peace and quiet, and it's private. You need a boat to get there."

"What do you mean she'd started staying there?"

"She rented it from me one weekend a month."

"How often?" I asked.

"Let's see ... I'd say about four times or so."

"And she never told you why she was going there?"

He shook his head. "No idea."

"How many bedrooms does it have?"

"Five."

"When was the last time she stayed there?"

"Four months ago, I think? I was kind of surprised."

"Why?"

"She had it booked for two more months, and she came into my office one day and canceled. I asked if she wanted to move the reservation to a different date, and she said no. She wouldn't be needing it again."

CHAPTER 34

What is your name?" the man asked.

The kid wiggled around in the rickety wooden chair, desperately trying to free himself. The man just sat back and watched, knowing no amount of effort on the kid's part would make a difference. The man had learned to tie knots at summer camp when he was a young boy. He'd even won an award for the best and fastest knot tied in camp, and a giant, red ribbon had been pinned to his chest. The kid wasn't going anywhere unless the man wanted him to, and right now, he didn't.

"You know," the man said. "I'm not sure why you're acting like you've been imprisoned. I don't have a weapon. I haven't hurt you. I'm only sitting here, trying to have a conversation. Man to ... well ... man to boy, it seems."

"If you just want to talk, why am I tied up?" the kid asked.

"I need you to stay put while I figure things out."

"Things? What *things?*"

"It depends on how you answer my questions." The man crossed one leg over the other. "Now then … where were we? Oh, right. You were about to tell me your name."

"Thomas Walker."

"I hear you also go by Tommy. Which would you prefer?"

"I don't care."

"Fine, then. Tell me, Thomas, what was the lady doing at your house today?"

"What lady?"

"Must I really define everything for you in order to get a decent response? I'm asking about the foreigner who has become chummy with the senator in recent days, or should I say, *former* senator. I'm sure you've seen the news. He stepped down today. It's about time."

"She said her name was Sloane. Can't remember her last name. She's not from here. She's American."

"Her last name is Monroe. Did she tell you her reason for being here?"

"She's helping the senator find the man responsible for the murders." The kid glared at the man. "I'm guessing that's you."

"It was always meant to be *murder*, singular—one simple, uncomplicated murder. Too bad things have to change sometimes, but the water has already boiled now. May as well make the most of it. Can I tell you a story?"

Tommy shrugged. "What for?"

"I'll take that as a yes," the man said. "Recently, I killed a woman, as you know. It was fast and clean and perfect, just like I intended. No prolonged suffering on her part. After she died, I stood back and looked at her. And do you want to know something? I actually felt all right about what I'd done. Satisfied. It was a real relief after a confusing few months. I went home pleased with myself, knowing I'd done the right—"

"Killing isn't right."

"Come now, Thomas. It's rude to interrupt a person before they've finished. Didn't your mum teach you any manners?"

"Don't talk about my mum."

"As you wish. Let's continue. After I returned home, something odd happened. Do you know of anything *odd* happening after she was murdered?"

Tommy shook his head.

The man smacked Tommy's knee. "Sure you do! But if you want to play dumb, that's fine. I'll indulge it for a moment. The morning after the murder, I turned on the news, interested to see what they had to say about the woman they'd found dead. I was shocked to learn the police were looking for a killer responsible for *two* homicides, not one. I thought surely there must have been a mistake. After she was dead, I'd left just as quickly as I came. No unnecessary victims, no screw-ups, and yet somehow, after I departed, a second person was murdered."

Tommy was quiet for a moment and then said, "Yeah, what about it?"

"Exactly my point, and that's why you're here. What about it, Thomas? You tell me. After all, you *know* what happened after I left, don't you?"

Tommy shook his head. "No, I don't. Why would I?"

The man leaned forward, gripping Tommy's kneecap in his hands. "Lie to me again, and I'll slit your throat right here, right now."

A tear ran down Tommy's cheek. The man loosened his grip and relaxed back into his seat again.

"I'll tell you how I *know* you're hiding something," the man said. "I *saw you* two nights before the murder. You crawled through a window on the side of the house. The next night, you did the same thing. I'm guessing on the night in question you arrived right after I left, which means you *know* what happened."

Tommy remained quiet.

"You do know, don't you?" the man asked. "Because all this

time, I've been trying to figure out why anyone would lie to the police about it. Why would they say I killed two people when I only killed one? It didn't make any sense at first, until I realized the second murder was being covered up. The boyfriend's murderer is being protected. What I want to know is—why?"

"You still killed Caroline, so why does it matter?"

The man slammed his fist down on the arm of the wooden chair. "Because. *I* didn't kill *him*! I had no reason to kill him. His death is not on me, and I won't be blamed for it!"

The man closed his eyes and took a few deep breaths, trying to collect himself. He didn't like getting angry. He didn't like it when he had a loss of control or how it made him feel inside.

"I apologize for the outburst," the man said. "I don't like to lose my temper. I really am a rational man, most of the time."

"If you say so."

"What's wrong with you, mentally?"

"Nothing is wrong with *me*. What's wrong with *you*?"

"Bold statement for such a soft kid. You're different, you and Grace. Your faces are similar and round, and your eyes remind me of almonds. Is that why you like Grace so much—because you both have eyes shaped like almonds?"

"Don't talk about her," Tommy said.

"Why not?"

"Just … don't."

"I might be able to respect your request *if* you give me the information I want. Part of my decision about what to do with you depends on your honesty. I'm giving you a chance not everyone gets with me, like your girlfriend's neighbor, the one who lived across the street. But then, she was a vile old woman, and you … well, the jury's still out on what you are, isn't it?"

Tommy's breathing changed, becoming heavier until he was puffing so hard through his cheeks, the man thought the kid might pass out. He'd pushed him, maybe a bit too far, but if it gave him the closure he wanted, it was worth it. Soon everything would be made right again. Soon everyone would know the truth.

"Do you need a glass of water or a moment alone to calm yourself down before we continue?" the man asked.

Tommy shook his head.

"I imagine you're getting hungry by now. I have a sandwich all made up for you. As soon as we're finished talking, you can have it."

"Don't hurt her."

"Don't hurt whom, your girlfriend?"

"Yes."

"I have no plans to do anything to her at the moment. The girl's just lost her mum. She's hurting enough, wouldn't you say?"

"All you want is for me to tell you who killed Hugh?"

The man nodded. "Spare no details. Tell me everything. You arrived at the house after I left that night, and then what happened?"

"I saw Grace."

"Where did you see her? What was she doing?"

"She was climbing out of her mum's bathroom window. She was crying. She said Caroline was dead and Hugh killed her. I ran into the house, and Grace chased after me. Hugh was standing outside Caroline's bedroom with his car keys in his hands. I thought he was leaving. Grace picked up the knife and started swinging it. Hugh ran, and she chased him. He got to the top of the stairs, and she swung at him and missed. He reached for the knife, trying to get it away from her, and I pushed him. I pushed him, and now he's dead."

The kid was bawling uncontrollably.

The man stroked his chin, thinking.

It was a good story.

But did he believe him?

"Get yourself together, Thomas, and stop sniveling. I have more questions. What happened after the two of you realized he was dead?"

"Grace said she was going to call her uncle. She said he'd know what to do. She told me to go home, and she'd call when it was safe."

"And did you leave like she asked?"

"No. I didn't want her to be alone. But then Grace's neighbor was running across the street toward the house. Grace told me if I didn't leave, it would make things worse, so I hid, but I didn't go home. I watched Grace to make sure she was okay."

"What did you see?"

"Grace told her neighbor that she killed Hugh. The neighbor hugged her. She said everything was going to be all right. They called James, and he came over. He told Grace not to worry. He said everything would be fine. Then I went home."

"You could have told the police what really happened. You could have told the truth, and you didn't."

"I wanted to protect Grace."

"And yourself. Now that I know the truth, you may as well admit it."

"I just did."

"I'm going to need you to admit it all over again. I'm going to record your confession."

"And then what's going to happen?"

The man drummed his fingers on the arm of the chair. "Hard to say. I'm feeling conflicted about what to do with you. Part of me thinks you deserve to die. The other part thinks you deserve to live to serve out whatever sentence you have coming to you. What to do, what to do … I suppose we could flip for it."

"Flip for it?"

"You know, heads or tails. I believe I have a coin in my car. Hold on. Be right back."

The man darted out the room, returning a minute later. He held the coin out in front of him, showing it to Tommy. "Got it. Now you call it."

Tommy's eyes widened. "You're crazy."

"All right, then. I'll call it. I choose the Queen."

The man pinched the coin in between his fingers and flipped it into the air, smiling when he clapped it flat against his hand as it came down.

"It's exhilarating, isn't it?" the man said. "Would you like to peek, or shall I?"

"I … I … don't …"

The man lifted his hand just enough to reveal the final verdict in the case of Thomas Walker. He stared at the coin for a moment, and then looked up and said, "Well, well, this is interesting."

CHAPTER 35

Tommy Walker had been missing for several hours. His cell phone had been found by the police, smashed to pieces in a supermarket parking lot not far from his home. If he had been taken, it wasn't hard to know who had him or why.

I was at Caroline's office, sitting at her desk, sifting through some papers I'd found in her top drawer, but it was just as James had said—nothing here provided me with the clues I so desperately needed. There were no client files. No notebooks. No hidden safe to break open.

Sitting in the same chair she had once sat in, I wondered how many patients had come through her door over the years and whether it was possible she'd angered one of them enough that he'd decided to end her life. Even more curious was the fact she'd been frequenting Brad's ocean rental in recent months.

Whom had she gone with, and what had she been doing there?

I had too many questions and too few answers.

The wall opposite Caroline's desk contained a shelf of nonfiction books with subjects spanning from anxiety and infidelity to abuse. Most of the books appeared to be in good condition, like they'd barely been touched. On the shelf below was another set of books, which were far more worn than the others. Even more interesting was the fact that all five of them were on the same subject: hypnotic regression.

I pulled one of the worn books off the shelf and flipped through it, learning that hypnotic regression was a way to assist the mind in traveling to different dimensions of time, or more easily understood, it dived into a person's past. A therapist using this technique could assist the patient with going back in his mind to a time where a specific event needed to be examined and worked through. The title page of the book had been signed in red pen by the author. It said: *Caroline, I hope this helps in your new research. Dean*

New research. Perhaps I'd found a clue after all.

I closed the book and inspected the cover. It was titled *Hypnotic Regression: From Unknown to Known*, and the author's name was D. Eugene Palmer.

I slid the book into my bag and headed outside. The street was dark and quiet. It appeared I was alone, and yet I couldn't help wondering if the murderer was out there, hiding in the trees, watching me as he had done in the past.

He could watch if he wanted.

I was watching too.

If he showed his face again, this time I'd be ready.

CHAPTER 36

I dreamed I was walking down an endless hall with numerous doors. As I passed each door, I stopped and knocked, but none of the doors ever opened, and all of them were locked. The hall I was in was an unfamiliar one, and it seemed my only way out was to keep knocking until one of the doors was opened. For now, I was trapped here.

I stood in the middle of the hall, wondering which door to try again, and then I heard a voice. Behind one of the doors, someone was talking to me.

"Sloane, are you in there? Are you awake?"

I sat straight up in bed, bouncing out of the dream into a state of mind where I was somewhat conscious. I realized someone was knocking on my front door. Through the darkness, I ran my hand across the side table. I flipped the clock around and glanced at the time. It was just after two a.m., and the voice on the opposite side of the door was Noel's. Worried what had him awake at this hour, I ran out of the bedroom to greet him.

I opened the door, finding him out of breath and panting on the other side.

"Are you all right?" I asked.

"I've been knocking for about five minutes. I started to think you weren't here, but I saw the car in the driveway and realized you must be. James has been trying to reach you."

I checked my phone. Noel was right. I had three missed calls.

"Why aren't you in bed?" I asked. "Is everything all right with Grace?"

"She's fine. I just looked in on her a few minutes ago. She's sleeping."

"What about James?"

"He's fine too."

"Why is he calling me so late?" I asked.

"The missing kid, the one who's sweet on Grace."

"Tommy Walker?"

Noel nodded. "He's been found."

CHAPTER 37

Instead of calling James, I went to the hospital to see him.

"Is it true?" I asked. "Is Tommy Walker alive?"

James nodded. "It's the strangest thing. He doesn't even have any injuries."

"What happened?"

"About an hour ago, a couple was taking a late-night stroll in the park. They heard a guy shouting for help, and when they ran over, they found Tommy sitting in a chair, tied to a tree. Want to take a guess at the exact location he was found?"

I didn't need to—somehow I already knew. "Where we were found?"

"Yep. When the police got to Tommy, a round metal serving platter with a lid was sitting on his lap, the kind you get from room service at a hotel. They lifted the lid and found a perfectly made fish sandwich and a note inside of a plastic bag sitting next to it."

"What was the quote this time?"

"It said: *Bait the hook well. This fish will bite.*"

Clever and annoying. "Was anything else found?"

"Inside the plastic bag with the note, there was also a recording device. The police played it. The only voice on the recording is Tommy's."

"What did he say?"

"It's a confession. He says *he* killed Hugh."

I stood there a moment and took it all in. "Could that be true?"

"I don't know. I have to talk to Grace. They're letting me out of here in the morning. Once I get home, I'll ask her."

"Where is Tommy now?"

"At the police station. Charlie is there with him. I've asked him to represent Tommy. He should be getting in touch with me soon to let me know the latest. All we can hope for now is that Tommy knows something that will lead us to this guy. I'm glad the kid's alive, but it doesn't make any sense. He let Tommy go, just like he let you go. Why spare some and kill others?"

I didn't know.

"Were you aware your sister was renting a place one weekend a month from Charlie's cousin?" I asked.

He shook his head. "I had no idea."

"She rented it for about four months and then had two additional months booked, but she canceled those a few months before she died."

"Around the time Evan Hall committed suicide."

"Looks like it."

"Well, I don't know anything about it. But about six months back, Caroline said she wanted Grace to start spending more time with the men in the family since she didn't have a father figure at home and felt it would benefit her since she was in her teens. So, here and there, she'd let Grace spend a weekend with either me or my father, but I didn't know Caroline was going out of town during that time."

"I'm trying to find out why she rented his place and what she was doing there."

"All right, let me know if you learn anything."

My thoughts turned to the killer. He was different than any other I'd tracked before. He was meticulous and precise and yet restless at the same time. He was forgiving and unforgiving. He seemed to have his own code of ethics, which he adhered to as long as it suited him. I was starting to think the killer might not be concerned about being caught. If there were a type of killer who had me worried, it was this guy because he wasn't a specific type.

He was unpredictable.

CHAPTER 38

Charlie Branson had large, dark circles under his eyes when he walked into James' hospital room.

James took one look at him and frowned. "That bad, huh?"

Charlie leaned against the wall, shook his head, and sighed. "Well, Tommy is sticking by his recorded confession. And now the police suspect him of killing Caroline as well."

"He didn't kill her, though," James said.

"*I* know that, and *you* know that," I said, "but think about it from a cop's perspective. Tommy conveniently showed up around the time of Caroline's murder and had been sneaking over to her house for weeks after being told he wasn't allowed to see Grace. To a cop, that's motive."

I had to hand it to the kid for being honest, if what he said was true.

James looked at Charlie. "What did he say about what happened that night?"

"He said when he got there, Grace told him Hugh had murdered Caroline, and he was trying to protect her. They chased Hugh to the top of the stairs. Tommy pushed Hugh, and he fell to his death. I believe him, but I'm not sure I have the entire story."

"At least we can assume Tommy was kidnapped," I said. "He didn't tie himself to that tree."

"There's something else," Charlie said, "and you're not going to like it, but there's little I can do to stop it from happening now that Tommy's talked to the police."

James shook his head. "No. They're *not* talking to Grace, especially without me there. She doesn't even know any of this has happened yet."

"I understand how you feel," Charlie said, "but at the very least Grace was an eyewitness. You can't protect her from this, James. Not this time."

"If Tommy is telling the truth, and he killed Hugh, and Grace told you and Adelaide that she lied to protect Tommy, she'll be heartbroken about it … but maybe it's for the best," I said. "This will finally get everything out in the open, and Grace can move on."

"Wait … what?" Charlie said. "What are you talking about?"

James clenched his jaw and glared at me, but with Tommy's confession, the time to protect Grace had passed. The jig was most definitely up.

"Don't be upset with me, James," I said. "Charlie represents your family, which means he represents Grace. He needs to know what's going on, and *we* need to figure out the best way to break the news to her about Tommy's arrest before the police do."

James looked at Charlie. "How long do we have?"

"They want to talk to Grace in the morning." He glanced at his watch. "We agreed on ten, and they're allowing me to drive her to the station."

"And me," James said. "I'll be going too."

"But you haven't been released from the hospital yet," Charlie said.

"I don't care. As of this moment, I'm releasing myself."

Charlie shrugged. "Okay. *We'll* take her in."

I thought about suggesting we make it a threesome, but I didn't.

"Tell me everything Tommy told the police about the guy who took him," James said. "I want to make sure we go into the meeting tomorrow with all of the necessary details."

Charlie nodded. "Tommy was at the grocery store, getting a few items for his mum. He came out and saw a guy parked a bit off the road, next to that pond on Cloud Street. Tommy walked by, and the guy was digging around in his trunk. He looked at Tommy and said there was something wrong with one of his tires. Since the tire in question was on the other side of the car, Tommy didn't go around to check and see if something was wrong with it or not. He just took the guy at his word. The guy told Tommy the spare tire was stuck and asked if he would give him a hand getting it out. As soon as Tommy poked his head into the trunk, the guy stuck a knife to Tommy's chest and told him not to make a sound. He said if he didn't comply, he'd push the knife into his chest, it would stop his heart, and he'd die instantly."

"What happened next?"

"The guy told Tommy to climb into the trunk. He said if Tommy behaved and didn't make a scene, he might not hurt him, or Tommy's mum, who the guy mentioned by name."

"He actually said the word *might*?" James asked. "I *might* not hurt you?"

Charlie nodded.

"What an arsehole," James said. "Preying on Tommy's emotions. Probably got his jollies off over it, too."

"It worked. Scared the shit out of him. He did what he was asked."

"Did Tommy say anything about the car?" I asked. "Inside? Outside? Color? Make? Model?"

"We know the car is black, vintage, and in perfect condition. Tommy said the car was shiny enough for him to see his reflection when he was standing outside of it, and that the trunk smelled like vanilla and honey."

"How long did they drive for?" I asked.

"He doesn't know. He was too freaked out. He tried counting while he was in the trunk to figure out how much time had passed, but he was so shaken up, he had to keep restarting."

"So the guy could have taken him anywhere," I said.

"I'm just telling you both what we know so far."

"Was the guy wearing a disguise?" I asked.

Charlie shook his head. "Hard to believe, but the guy didn't mask his face or anything. You would think this would be a major break in the case. But the hard thing is Tommy hasn't been great on a lot of details."

"What happened when they arrived where they were going?" James asked.

"Once Tommy heard the guy kill the engine on the car, he had a moment of bravery. The guy opened the trunk, and Tommy started kicking him. The guy got verbally aggressive and shut the trunk, leaving Tommy to wait it out. He returned to the car several minutes later, told Tommy to get out of the car, and they walked into the house together. He put Tommy in one of the bedrooms, locked him in, and said he'd be back."

"Did Tommy say anything about what the house looked like? Did he recognize the area they were in?"

"The house was surrounded by rainforest on all sides. It was a single level and made of wood paneling of some kind. There was a greenhouse off to one side with a bunch of stuff growing in it, and off to the other side was a two-car garage. It was open, and another car was parked there. It was red, small, and round in shape, similar to a Toyota Prius. It looked new."

"What did Tommy say about the inside of the house?" I asked.

"It was clean. Everything was in its place. Minimal furniture, neutral colors. A record player was playing opera music in the background. While Tommy was in the room, he heard the guy talking to someone in the kitchen, but he was too far away to hear the actual conversation."

"Could he tell whether it was a man or a woman?"

Charlie shook his head.

"What did the guy who took him look like?" I asked.

"Tommy is sure they are the same height because he said he could look right into the guy's eyes when he stood in front of him. He described the guy as 'old,' but when police asked how old, Tommy said 'about as old as you.' The cop he was talking to is forty-nine. We know the guy has salt-and-pepper hair and blue eyes, but Tommy didn't notice any distinguishing features that set him apart from anyone else. He said he looked like every other guy that age."

I shook my head. The lack of details was frustrating, but at the same time, it was better than anything we knew so far.

"What was the man wearing?" I asked.

"All black. Tommy said he looked like he was dressed to work in an office, but not as a worker—more like as a manager or someone in charge."

"So we're looking for a murderer who's clean-cut and professional-looking," I said. "His taste in music, the fish dish he made, and the Shakespeare references tell me he's clever, and most likely has above-average intelligence, or he perceives himself as someone who is intelligent and enjoys the finer things in life. He's efficient at using a knife, so I'd guess he either works in the medical field now or in the past or has some kind of medical training, which may even be self-taught, but I'd lean toward actual classes … a skill set he's picked up from somewhere."

Charlie stared at me for a moment. "There is one other thing I need to mention."

"What is it?" I asked.

"The kidnapper asked about you, Sloane. He wanted to know all about you."

It didn't come as a shock to me at all.

"What about me?"

"He was most interested in why you're here and what you were doing at Tommy's house."

"And did Tommy tell him?"

"He did, which means you need to be even more careful. There's a good chance he'll come after you again."

And this time, he wouldn't be generous enough to let me go. I didn't fit his moral sense of murder before. Now, I probably did, and he'd have come up with a justified reason to kill me—self-preservation, the most basic of human instincts, the very reason we survive.

"I expected this to happen," I said. "Was anything else discussed between them?"

"The kidnapper's main interest in taking Tommy was to find out what really happened the night he killed Caroline and why he had been blamed for a murder he didn't commit."

"Why is this guy so fixated on this?" James asked.

"If his murders are predicated on the moral high ground he's set for himself," I said, "he may see what he's doing as ethical, just, and good. What happened to Hugh isn't something he sanctioned."

"Hugh wasn't a great person, though," Charlie said.

"The killer might not know that."

"So, in the end, after Tommy gave the guy all the information he had, the killer just let him go?" James asked.

"He flipped a coin and told him one side he lived, the other he died."

James shook his head. "The guy's crazy. He's absolutely crazy."

"He stuck to his word, though," I said.

"Tommy won the coin toss," Charlie said. "Afterward the man gave him a sandwich, put him back in the trunk, and drove him to the city. He took him to the same spot where you two were found, waited until it was quiet, tied him up, staged the scene, and told Tommy to count to fifty. When he got to fifty, he could scream, but if he screamed too early, the man promised he'd come back and end his life for good. Tommy counted to one hundred just to be safe. He was found, and now we're here."

CHAPTER 39

I stood in the doorway, watching James bend down next to Grace's bed. He smoothed a hand across her cheek, and her eyes fluttered open. She threw her arms around him and smiled.

"You've been gone a long time," she said, "like forever and ever."

"I know," James said. "I'm sorry. Can you forgive me?"

She looked around him at me and said, "I liked the hamburger you brought me."

"I'm glad," I said.

She pointed at the sack in my hand. "What's in the bag? Another burger?"

"It will be an ice-cream sundae once you put it together."

Her eyes widened. "For breakfast?"

I nodded. "Your uncle said it was okay."

She threw her blanket to the side and hopped out of bed. "Okay, let's make them. Let's make them right now!"

The three of us walked to the kitchen, and I spread the topping options on the counter. Grace chose what she wanted and moved them to one side.

"Do you want to make it, or do you want me to?" I asked.

"You can do it," she said. "You're having one too, right?"

"Not right now," I said. "Maybe later."

She looked me up and down. "Oh, come on. We didn't get to eat the burgers together. And ... uhh ... you're too skinny. Are you eating?"

Not enough. Since I'd arrived, I'd probably lost five, maybe ten pounds. Some people ate to feel better when dealing with stress. I fasted. Not because I wanted to, but because my stomach tended to reject food when it was in knots.

I stared at her, realizing it didn't matter what I wanted or didn't want right now or that food didn't sound appetizing. The only thing that mattered right now was *her*.

"You're right, I do need it," I said. "How about I make yours and you make mine? Put in whatever you like, just don't make it too big, okay?"

She nodded and opened the lid to the ice cream. "What's the catch?"

"What do you mean?"

"I've never been allowed to have dessert for breakfast before, not even on my birthday."

"Well, you do today."

I glanced outside. James and Noel were talking on the back patio. James was coming clean about everything he hadn't told his father. While I made Grace's sundae, I'd stolen a few glances outside. James looked apologetic and sheepish, unlike the person he had been before his life melted down. Noel looked like he needed an air vent in his head so he could let the steam out. James talked, and Noel threw his hands in the air, shouting at James and scolding him.

Grace ignored it at first, and then when she'd had enough, she hopped off her chair and walked to the sliding glass door. She pulled it open and said, "Stop it. Stop fighting. You can't be angry when you eat ice cream. Ice cream is for happy people, and if you can't be happy, you can't have any. Got it?"

James and Noel looked at each other, and their debate stopped. They walked into the house, but the tension that remained between them was thick, clinging to the air like a dense fog that refused to be lifted. And yet, in her best interest, they'd agreed to an unspoken truce. The harsh words could wait for now. Grace quickly whipped up two more sundaes for the boys.

We sat at the counter and dove into the ice cream, and for a moment James, Noel, and Grace seemed to put away their cares and remember what life was like when it was simple, at a time when Caroline was still alive and they were an entire family again.

When the bowls were empty, James looked at the time and sighed. Grace was due at the police station in less than an hour. If he was going to prep her for what was to come, it had to be now.

"Well, that was good," Grace said. "What should we do next? Can we go to the trampoline place?"

James looked at Grace and smiled. "Do you remember the talk we had about Hugh?"

At the mention of Hugh's name, Grace shoved her hands in between her legs. "Uhh … which one?"

"The one where I told you not to talk to anyone else about what really happened."

She looked at me and then at Noel. "But … I thought you said …"

"It's okay, Grace," James said. "They both know."

Grace bowed her head. "Oh."

"I shouldn't have told you not to talk about it to anyone," he said. "I was wrong."

She shrugged. "It's okay."

"No, sweetie, it isn't. It's better to talk things out, and it's better to tell the truth."

She stared into her empty bowl. "Oh … kay."

"We all care about you. Sloane and Grandpa want to help as much as I do."

Grace looked at Noel. "You're mad at me, aren't you?"

He grabbed her hand, rubbing the outside with his fingers. "Of course I'm not mad, darlin'. I could never be mad at such a brave girl. I know what happened the night your mum died is hard. No matter what, I'll always be proud of you."

"No, you won't. I saw you outside. What I did was wrong, and you know it."

"I wasn't mad at you. I was mad at your uncle for not telling me before now. It's never good to hold a lie inside."

"It can be, sometimes," she said.

"Not this time."

"Why not?"

"Sometimes we want to protect the person we care about because we love them. I did that once when your grandma was still alive."

"You *lied* to Grandma?"

Noel nodded.

"Did she ever find out?" Grace asked.

"She did. When she realized I'd been keeping something from her, it hurt her more than if I would have just told her the truth in the first place. You understand what I'm trying to say, don't you?"

She gave a slight nod, and I tensed, knowing what was coming next.

"Is there anything you have lied about that you want to confess?" Noel asked. "It doesn't matter what it is. We won't be mad. We're all here to protect you."

Grace let go of Noel's hand and began rocking back and forth. "I … I guess so. There *is* one thing."

"Will you tell us what it is?" Noel asked.

"I … guess I could tell you. It's about Tommy."

"What about Tommy?"

This was it. The moment she revealed what she hadn't been able to say before. The moment she released herself from the burden she'd been carrying over the past few weeks, so she could begin healing.

"Tommy used to come to my room at night after Mum went to bed," she said. "It was only because she said he couldn't come over. He missed me, and I missed him. I know it was wrong, but I like him so much. Please don't be mad."

It wasn't the confession we'd hoped for.

"And?" Noel asked. "Is there anything else?"

"He slept next to me in bed. He just wanted to make sure I was all right. And Mum wouldn't let me see him, and I know it was wrong, and now she's dead, and she can never forgive me for what I did."

"Tommy's a good person," Noel said. "Your mum knew it too."

"How do you know she did?"

"She told me. She was just worried about you because you're growing up so fast, and she wasn't ready. She was going to let you start seeing him again."

Grace's eyes widened. "She was?"

Noel nodded. "I appreciate your honesty. Is there anything *else* you haven't told us?"

She raised a brow, looking at Noel, and then James, and then me. "Uhh … nope. Do *you guys* have anything to tell me?"

Even now, she remained steadfast as Tommy's protector.

"Grace," James said. "Did Tommy push Hugh down the stairs?"

"I already told you. I did it. Why would you say that?"

James paused, and I could tell he was trying to decide how to word his next statement. He started with, "I don't want you to worry about what I'm going to say."

"I am worried because you told me not to worry, which makes me worried."

"This morning, Tommy told the police he was at the house the night your mum died. He said he pushed Hugh, not you."

Grace's face went still, like she'd just been paralyzed.

"Did you just hear what I said?" James asked.

No response. No movement. She didn't even blink.

James placed a hand on Grace's shoulder. "Grace, did you hear me? Did you hear what I just said?"

"Where is Tommy?" she asked. "Where is he right now? I need to talk to him."

"He's with the police, I believe. I can call and find out."

When James didn't take his cell phone out fast enough, Grace huffed in frustration.

"Why aren't you calling yet?" she asked. "Hurry up."

James grabbed his phone. "I'll do it right now, all right?"

He left the room and returned a minute later.

"Well?" Grace asked.

"He's still at the police station."

"I don't understand."

"They can't just let him go."

"Yes, they can, because Tommy's wrong. He didn't do it. I did."

"Grace," James said, "I know how much you care about Tommy. But you don't need to protect him anymore."

"I'm not protecting anyone!" she yelled. "I don't want him to be locked up with bad people who do bad things. He's not bad. I don't want him to go to jail."

"And I don't want *you* to go to jail."

"I don't care what you want anymore. I don't care about any of it. I want to talk to the police. I want to talk to them now."

"We will, but first I think we should—"

"No, Uncle James. I want to talk to the police ... right ... now."

She stepped off the stool, grabbed a long, black cardigan sweater off the back of the chair, and wrapped it around her nightgown. "I'm ready. Let's go."

"Now just a minute. Grace," James said. "You need to get ready, and we haven't finished talking about this. There's more I need to—"

"I'm ready, and I'm done talking."

She walked outside, slamming the door behind her, and for a moment, the three of us sat in silence, stunned at what just happened and realizing we no longer knew what to believe anymore.

CHAPTER 40

While James and Noel accompanied Grace to the police station, I hung back and watched the surveillance video James had taken from Caroline's house on the night she died. James was right. The video showed a terror-stricken Grace running out of the house with bloodstained hands, but even after rewinding, pausing, and watching it again and again, I never saw even the slightest hint of the killer or of Tommy.

I grabbed the book on hypnotic regression, searched the internet for Dean Eugene Palmer, and found his website. He was in his sixties and lived in Sydney with his wife and their five dogs. I sent him a brief email, mentioned Caroline's murder, and gave him my number, asking if it was possible to speak by phone.

Next I searched the name *Evan Hall*, the boy whose obituary I'd found inside Caroline's jewelry stand. It took some digging, but I located the names and addresses of his parents. According to the internet, they owned two homes, were still married, and were in their early seventies. I jotted down both addresses and tried to wake myself up with a cup of coffee—on a day like this, there was no chance tea would come close to cutting it.

Then I hit the road.

The first address took me to a building of condominiums. I found the right one and knocked, but it seemed no one was home. The second residence was a much farther drive. About forty-five minutes later, I arrived to find a modest, older house with a roof that looked like it leaked when it rained and a car in the driveway that may have still been running but was made of spare parts. One of the tires was even a different size than the others. Even though there were many visual imperfections, the deck on the side of the house was perfectly clean and lined with a stunning array of tropical plants and flowers. There was a bright, striped hammock on one end and a wicker seating area on the other, which offered impeccable views of the rainforest.

The front door opened, and a sizable woman stepped out. She had a pleasant face, rosy cheeks, and a smile that warmed my insides.

"Hello," she said. "Are you the delivery woman?"

I shook my head. "I'm looking for the parents of Evan Hall."

"I'm Beth. I was his mum. And you are?"

Complicated, on a good day.

I did my best to explain why I was there, without making the story too overwhelming to understand. I stuck to how I knew Caroline and that I'd found Evan's obituary while going through her things following her death.

"Caroline was a nice woman, from what I understand," Beth said. "Evan spoke highly of her. That's why we asked her to speak at his funeral."

"How did Evan know Caroline? Was she his therapist?"

Beth placed a hand on her hip and stared at me as if trying to decide what to say, making me realize I'd led into my more aggressive questions a bit too soon. I needed to take a step back for a moment.

To climb steep hills requires a slow pace at first.

Great.

Now *I* was quoting Shakespeare.

"Would you like to come in?" she asked.

I nodded, switched off the faucet to my mouth, and followed her.

"Pardon the outside of this place," she said, "and some of the inside too. I haven't been able to keep up on things since my husband was injured trying to replace the doors. He was carrying them all himself. Can you believe it?"

"Sorry to hear he was injured."

"This was our son's house. We own it, though. We've been here for a week now, cleaning up and getting it ready to go on the market. We tried coming out sooner, but neither of us had the heart to be here. We still don't, but every month that passes there's more work to be done than the month before, so we decided it was time to deal with it before it falls into even more disrepair."

As she spoke, tears formed in her eyes. She attempted to laugh and wiped them away, but her suffering was evident.

"I'm sorry," she said. "I know I should be stronger. It's just … Evan was our son, our *only* child, and we never thought we'd outlive him. I don't think parents ever plan on outliving their children. It shouldn't be that way."

It was the kind of moment where most people, whether they were familiar with one another or not, did things like reach out and give the other person a hug. I smiled and patted her on the back, a gesture suitable to my comfort level.

"I lost someone I care about not long ago," I said. "She was like a daughter to me. I still think about her every day."

"You know my pain, then."

"I do."

We walked into the living room and sat down. On the mantle was a photo of a man I assumed was Evan. He was sitting on the same couch I was on now, holding a cat. His thick, chestnut-color hair was tucked beneath a hat, but what struck me most were his eyes. They were dark and sad, like he was completely lost in them.

I pointed to the photo. "Your son was very handsome."

She nodded. "We bought him the shirt he's wearing for his thirty-fourth birthday, which took place a few months before he died. He wore the shirt all the time. Ah well. Can I offer you a snack? I've just taken some biscuits out of the oven."

Biscuits, I had learned, were cookies.

"No, thank you," I said.

"What about a beverage?"

"Sure. Can I have a—"

I was about to ask for water when she winked at me and said, "Vodka or gin? I don't have a lot here, but I have mixers."

When I first arrived, her speech had seemed a bit slurred, which I'd assumed might have been a speech impediment. It seemed I was mistaken. It was the middle of the day, and she was sitting in a home that stirred up painful memories. She didn't look like someone who took to the bottle on a regular basis, but today, and I expect many other days of late, she had treated herself to some liquid courage to get through it all. If I hadn't driven and didn't need to keep my wits about me, I probably would have joined her.

"I'd just like some water," I said. "If that's okay."

"Sure it is. Be right back."

She shuffled out of the room and returned with one glass full of water and another glass only a quarter of the way full, which looked like water, but probably wasn't. She handed my glass to me, swallowed half of the contents of hers, and plopped it on the table, staring down at it like she was tempted to polish it off and make another.

"My son sought help from Caroline for depression," she said, "which I believe he suffered from because of an issue in his past that he never quite came to terms with, even as an adult."

"Can I ask what happened?"

She nodded. "When he was ten years old, he was climbing a tree with a couple other kids. One of the kids, Randy, had a fear of heights and didn't want any part of going up the tree like Evan had. But Evan was a charming little fellow at that age, and he convinced Randy to do it anyway. About three-quarters of the way up, Randy panicked and started to cry. Evan slid down and held his hand out to him. Randy reached for it, but before he could take it, he fell out of the tree."

"Did Randy survive the fall?"

"He did, but he would have been better off if he hadn't. He's still alive now, but he hit his head so hard when he fell, he has permanent brain damage. Poor thing doesn't know his left from his right, and Evan never forgave himself for what happened."
I crossed one leg over the other, taking in everything she'd just said. "Do you think Evan ended his life because he couldn't live with the memory of it anymore?"

She pursed her lips for a moment, then said, "I told you before that Evan was fond of Caroline, but I wasn't sure how I felt about her myself."

"What do you mean?" I asked.

"When he first went to her, he seemed better."

"How so?"

"For the first time in his life, he was letting go of the past, starting to move on, creating a real life for himself. He asked us to help him buy this house. We were thrilled."

"What changed?"

"Caroline's treatment of him changed. She talked him into doing a few sessions with her where he went back into his past and faced what happened. She said it would help him move forward, but it didn't. It did just the opposite."

"These sessions, did he call it regression therapy?"

She nodded. "I believe that's right, yes."

"Did he ever tell you how it worked?"

"He didn't like talking about the details of what went on, so I don't know much more than what I've just told you."

"These meetings ... were they held at her office?"

"I don't think so. They were in a house somewhere on the beach."

Brad's house.

I found it strange that Caroline was hosting private weekend sessions away from the office, and I was starting to wonder if her services with Evan included a lot more than just therapy. Perhaps it wasn't therapy at all. Perhaps Caroline had started seeing Evan in a personal, romantic way, and they had to meet somewhere in secret. As much as I didn't want to think it was possible, I didn't have a better explanation at the moment.

"Did you think it was odd that your son went somewhere other than Caroline's office as part of his therapy?" I asked.

"I did, at first. And I said something to Evan about it."

"What did he say?"

"He said he wasn't alone. There were others there with him."

"How many?"

"I don't know the exact number. He never told me. I don't think it was a lot. Two or three maybe?"

A group therapy session. That explained the need to rent a place with five bedrooms.

"The last session they had was right before Evan's suicide," she said. "All I know is he left that weekend in a good mood, but when he came back, it was like all of the time he'd spent in therapy had been for nothing. His depression returned, and it was worse than before. He clammed up and wouldn't talk to me about it. Wouldn't say a single word. He just locked himself up in this house and shut the rest of the world out."

"Did he ever mention the names of anyone else in the group?"

She shook her head. "If he did, it wouldn't have meant anything."

"Why not?"

"They didn't go by their real names. Everyone in the group session made up a name for themselves—which I found silly, to be honest. It was what Caroline wanted, apparently. She thought it would protect their privacy in the real world, but this isn't a big city."

"What name did Evan use?"

"He didn't feel like making one up, so he went by his middle name, Peter, and then the first time they all got together someone else in the group said he looked more like a Petey than a Peter, and from then on, the name just stuck, and that's what they called him."

CHAPTER 41

The man sat inside his car, listening to it idle and tapping his fingers on the steering wheel, thinking about what to do next. It was clear Sloane Monroe wasn't going to relent, wasn't going to stop searching until she'd found him. In a way, he admired the tenacity and drive she had to do what she thought was right. It showed integrity and strength of character.

For this reason, there was merit in sparing her life.

But she had become involved in something that wasn't her business, and although she was a private investigator who sought people out for a living, it was something she was paid to do, it seemed to him that she did it for monetary gain and not because she had a personal investment or concern for those affected by what she was doing.

For this reason, she had to die.

And die she would.

He glanced in his rearview mirror. "What do you think, Petey? Should I spare her today and kill her tomorrow or shall I kill her today and be done with it?"

Petey rolled his eyes.

"Are you tired of me talking about her?" the man asked. "Is that it? Maybe if I wasn't always talking to myself these days and you joined in the conversation for once, you could have a say in the topics up for discussion."

Petey remained silent, as he always did, staring out the window like he was bored. "When we get home, you should consider changing your shirt this time. You've been wearing that tired, worn red shirt for months, even though I've repeatedly asked you to change. It's rude, you know? I try to give you some advice, as your friend, and you don't seem to care."

The man watched Sloane's car pull out of the driveway of the house Petey lived in. He wondered what she'd talked to his parents about. It seemed he was always wondering when it came to her. An idea crossed his mind. Perhaps if he wanted to *know* what she knew, he should ask.

CHAPTER 42

For the first time in days, I felt like I was making a different kind of progress, the kind that was getting me close to the man I was hunting. About ten miles down the road, I discovered I had a travel buddy, a small red car that turned when I turned and really wasn't hiding the fact he was tagging along, either. It was late afternoon on an open, public road, and one thing was certain: he *wanted* me to see him.

What I hadn't decided was what I was going to do about it.

Winding my way back down to the city, I spied a place to pull over. It wasn't the most public location, but it was public enough for now. Right before I pulled to the side, I second-guessed myself, deciding to wait just a little longer and see what became of my tagalong. I kept going.

I put my phone on speaker and called James.

"I'm on my way back from visiting with the parents of Evan Hall," I said, "and someone's following me."

"Who's following you?" James asked.

"I'm not sure. Might be our killer. Might be someone else. Whoever it is, he's not trying to hide the fact that he's tailing me."

"What do you mean? What is he doing?"

"He speeds up and gets within inches of my car, and then he backs off. A couple minutes go by, and he does the same thing again."

"Is he trying to run you off the road?"

"No, not yet. I think he wants me to pull over."

"Where are you?"

I gave him my location.

"You're still at least twenty-five minutes away from the city," he said. "Do *not* pull over."

"How fast can you get here?"

"I've just dropped Grace at the house to have lunch with my sister. Dad's with me. He'll call the police and give them your location. For now, stay on the phone and keep coming down the hill. We're heading your way now."

It was a good plan, but it was also safe. If the killer was in tow, this was my opportunity to face him.

"I'm pulling over," I said.

"What? No!"

"I'll keep the call active so you can hear what's going on. If it's him, I need to do this."

James was yelling into the phone, but his words washed out, like he was speaking to me through a tunnel. My heart was racing too fast to focus on him. I needed to focus on me now ... and on the moment. I pulled the car to the side, and a man pulled alongside me. He put his window down. I shushed James and did the same.

"Stay in the car," I said to the man. "If your door opens, or if you make any movement to come near me, I'm gone."

I revved my engine to make sure he received the message.

He nodded. "As you wish, Detective."

I lunged for the glove box and opened it.

"Don't bother with the gun," the man said. "It's no longer loaded."

I reached for it anyway. He was right. It was empty.

For an assumed killer, he certainly didn't look the part, not that all killers looked the same. They didn't. But most had similar eyes, wild and hungry, eyes that always looked more dead than alive. His face was hidden, his eyes covered by dark glasses and his head by a dark-gray fedora. He looked clean and polished, like a well-groomed politician about to sway me with a moving speech. He was mid-forties, I guessed, and slender, with dark, short hair. Most of it was tucked under his hat.

"Have you finished?" he asked.

"Finished what?" I asked.

"Critiquing me." He smiled. "I've seen you, and now you've seen me. What do you think? Do I fit your mold?"

"I don't think anything yet."

"Sure you do. You look confused, Detective. Are you wondering why my cookie doesn't fit into your cutter?"

"I'm wondering what you want," I said. "Why were you trying to get me to pull over?"

"I want to talk, of course."

"All right, let's talk."

"And here I was thinking you would have so many questions I might not get a word in."

"I do. They can wait."

He shook his head. "Ladies first. Go ahead—ask what you will."

I decided to go straight for the jugular.

"Why did you kill Caroline?"

"You know the answer to that question now, don't you? She killed Petey. Only some people never actually die, do they? I've come to realize they return to us in one form or another. I have to say, I never believed there was life after death until now. I always assumed we all became one with the earth again, dust scattering in the wind after we're dead. I was wrong."

He glanced in his rear-view mirror. I looked around, didn't see anything.

"Caroline didn't kill Petey," I said. "He committed suicide."

"There's where you're wrong. She put thoughts into his mind, ideas that made him see himself for who he was instead of who he wished to be. I really believe she thought she was helping him, but she pushed too far, you see. She could have stopped, but she didn't. She pressed on, doing irreversible damage. It was wrong. Unethical. I told her as much, and all she kept saying was she knew what she was doing, and we all needed to trust her. She pretended like she was trying to help, but the only one she was helping was herself … to further her own career."

"Why do you think that? What was she doing at the house on the ocean?"

He raised a brow. "Oh, I see. Now, this is interesting. You haven't learned everything about her yet, have you?"

"Tell me what I don't know."

"That would be too easy. It would rob you of the chance to seek it out for yourself. I have no intention of spoiling it for you. You're so close."

"Why didn't you kill me when you had the chance?" I asked. "You killed Adelaide, and yet you spared me. You killed Caroline, and yet you spared Tommy. What makes you decide to kill one person and not the other?"

He frowned. "I made a mistake with you."

"By keeping me alive, you mean?"

"I suppose so, yes. But then again, maybe not. I quite enjoy this conversation."

"And Tommy?" I asked.

"Has the little sparrow started to sing?"

"He's confessed to the murder of Hugh, just like you wanted."

"Well then, there's your answer." His gaze shifted from me to his wrist. "You have four minutes left. Better make the most of it."

"Why only four?"

"I saw your mouth moving before, while you were driving. You were talking to someone. Is he there now, listening to our conversation? What are you worried about? That something might happen to you if you don't have a lifeline to depend on? Do you fear I'd finish the job and kill you this time? I'm giving you the chance to talk to me before *they* get here. One chance, that's all. Don't blow it. I'll disappear long before they arrive, and they'll never find me."

"They'll find you, and if they don't, *I* will."

"This area has many back roads, and I know all of them. So, what is it you want to know?"

"What's your name?" I asked.

"Be smart, Detective."

"All right. Where do you work? What do you do? Was Caroline the first person you ever killed?"

"Next question."

"When you stabbed Caroline, you were precise. She died right away. Do you have medical training? Do you work in the medical field?"

"Rapid-fire questions. I appreciate your enthusiasm."

"And yet, so far you've been unwilling to answer."

"Keep going. Three minutes."

"Were you in a special therapy group with Evan Hall that Caroline started?"

He nodded.

"How many others in the program?"

"Three. Well, including Petey and myself, five. Two minutes."

As he counted down, I thought about what I could do to stall him.

"What was the purpose of the program?"

"Read the book and find out."

"What book?" I asked.

"The book tucked inside your handbag."

"What are the names of the others in the program?"

"What an unethical question."

"Are you done killing?" I asked.

"Regrettably, no. I don't think so."

"Who's your next target?"

"You, for starters, and then I suppose I should tie up loose ends. It's unfortunate the senator survived. I'm still not certain how, although you were a most unwelcome distraction at the time. One inch less, and the man lived. I'm sure you're proud of yourself for that."

"To see him live and you fail? Very."

"One minute, and now it's my turn. Why did you come all this way to help a man you barely even know find a person you know nothing about?"

"It's what I do."

"You admit you took the job for the money, then?"

"Nothing I do is ever *just* a job. I go after men like you to stop you from doing more harm than you already have."

"*Wrong.* You go after men like me to fill a void in your own life. You go after men like me because you're afraid if you don't, your life will lack the luster you so desperately seek. Take away the thrill of the chase, and your life has no meaning. I fulfill something in you. Something dark and disturbing. Something you don't want anyone else to see or know about. You don't just *want* to find me, you ache when you don't."

"You're wrong," I said. "You know nothing about me or my life."

He bent his head toward me. "I never took you for a liar. At any rate, we'll have to agree to disagree for now because your time is up."

"You have no regrets over what you've done, do you?"

"I don't think about it much, one way or the other." He paused a moment. "Well, I suppose that's not true. I don't care about what others think about what I've done. All that matters is what I think of myself and whether I can justify my own actions. So far, I can."

He tipped his head toward me, and as his window went back up, he said, "You've made your choice to stay, and I accept it. When next we meet again, it will be the end ... for one of us."

CHAPTER 43

The man pulled back onto the road. I slipped in behind him, and the chase was on.

"Did you hear all that?" I asked.

"Every word," James said. "We recorded it."

"You wouldn't happen to recognize his voice?"

"I don't think so."

"I have his license plate number."

"Good work. Give it to me."

I gave it to him.

"I'll pass it along," he said. "See what we can find out."

"How's Grace? What happened?"

"She's fine, for now. I'll fill you in later. We're still several minutes away. Where are you right now?"

"On the road again. He's in front of me."

"Be careful, Sloane."

"Always."

No sooner had the word left my lips than the man made a sharp, right-hand turn, his car diving into what appeared to be nothing but a grove of trees. I jerked the car around and circled back, entering where he had. In front of me was a dirt road. I followed it for a couple of minutes, but there was no sign of his vehicle anywhere. A minute later, the road came to an abrupt end.

I got out of the car, scanning the area, but saw nothing.

I was empty-handed.

He was in the wind.

CHAPTER 44

I came across James and Noel on the road, and we followed each other back to the police station, a place I was sure James wasn't excited to be so soon after he'd left. Before we had entered the station, James wondered whether it might be better to tell the police about my conversation with the killer instead of playing the recording. He worried that revealing who I really was to the police and what I did for a living would land me in hot water. I assumed it would. But audible evidence of the killer's actual voice was too good not to share, especially if there was a chance he could be identified.

I was returned to the same room I'd been questioned in before. Charlie Branson was on one side of me, and James and Noel were on the other. A man I'd seen at Adelaide's crime scene walked in and introduced himself as Detective Miller. He was around Noel's age and a bear of a man, with a huge, square face, impressive dimples, and a short, messy crew cut. He was tall, six foot six, at least, and had the kind of hands he could easily grip a basketball in each.

He sat down across from me.

"You should have been honest with us about your reasons for being here from the start, Mrs. Monroe," Miller said. "You lied."

"She didn't lie," Charlie said.

"Withholding information is the *same* as lying," Miller said.

"Cut the crap, Miller," Noel said. "If Sloane wasn't around, we wouldn't even be sitting here right now. I've dealt with enough in the last few days. Cut her a break."

"I respect you, Noel, and all the years you worked here," Miller said, "but I can't just—"

Noel leaned forward. "You *can* and you *will*. I haven't asked for a whole lot since your investigation began, but I'm asking for this. Try living through the hell I am right now and then look me in the eye and tell me you wouldn't use every resource at your disposal to put this guy down. She's put herself in danger more than once searching for this guy, and that's worth something."

Miller leaned back in his chair, clasping his hands together behind his head. "Yeah, well, I still don't like it."

"I can live with that," Noel said. "Now, I don't care who you share the audio with, but keep Sloane's name out of it."

"How am I supposed to involve anyone else if I don't—"

"Say she's under police protection, and her information can't be revealed. I think we'd both agree that it's better to keep her identity a secret for now. You don't even have to modify it. The guy didn't use her name in the audio."

Miller pointed at me. "I don't want to hear your name come up again, understand? You should go home."

He'd said I *should* go home, instead of ordering me to go home.

"I'll protect Sloane's anonymity for now under one condition," Miller said.

"Name it," James said.

"I want to talk to Sloane alone, without you two, Noel and James, and without the lawyer."

"No way," James said. "If you want us to leave, fine. But Charlie stays."

"This isn't a negotiation."

"Sure it is. You just proposed a condition, and I've countered with ours."

No one had asked my opinion on the matter, and I sat there, listening to them duke it out as to who had the bigger ego. If I had talked, they would have drowned out anything I had to say. I saw only one solution. I stood up and walked out of the room.

Noel chased after me.

"Where are you going?" he asked.

"It's my decision whether I talk to Miller alone," I said.

"We're just making sure you're protected."

"You're all missing the point. I'm *not* protected, not anymore. The killer made it clear he's coming after me. Miller seems bright enough to understand it would be a mistake to send me packing. So, let's hear what it is he has to say."

CHAPTER 45

Miller sat across from me with a pleased look on his face. "I'd like to know what information you've come across in your own investigation that we may not know."

"That's not really why you want to see me alone, though," I said. "Is it?"

"It's not the only reason. We'll get to my agenda in a minute."

We swapped notes, except on his end, he didn't reveal anything I didn't already know. It didn't mean he lacked more information on his end. It just meant he wasn't willing to share it with me.

"What are your thoughts on the killer seeking you out to talk to you?" he asked.

"I'm not sure."

"You must have some idea why he did it."

"You heard what he said on the recording. Maybe I interest him, or maybe he needed to make contact in order to justify killing me, or maybe it's some other reason entirely."

"What do you think about him threatening to kill you?"

"I believe he means to do it."

"I'll tell you something I haven't shared with anyone else yet."

"Okay."

"We ran the guy's plates. They're registered. They're just not registered to him."

"How can you be sure?"

"The plates are registered to Evan Hall. And he's—"

"Dead," I said.

"Exactly."

Miller's idea of "sharing something" was more of him sharing nothing. It was information I couldn't do anything with, even though I assumed he didn't see it that way. He was gearing me up for something. I thought about the look on James' face when he'd left the room minutes before. He was worried. He had a right to be.

"Even with the recording, we still can't identify this guy," Miller said. "We're looking into what we can on the guy's car based on your description, but for now, we know little more than we did before this happened."

I leaned forward, resting my arms on the table. "I'm a big fan of being direct."

"Meaning?"

"You asked to see me alone for a reason. Why not tell me what it is? I'm aware of your desperation to catch this guy before he kills anyone else. And before you fume over the word I just used, we're desperate too, all of us, to put an end to it. If the killer is a man of his word, and I believe he is, he'll come for me. If that means you need to offer me up as the sacrificial lamb, I get it."

He stared at me for a moment.

"Unless I'm wrong," I said, "and you wanted to talk about something else?"

He shook his head. "You're exactly right. I was just about to ask you if you'd consider being the bait."

I stood. "I already am the bait, so I'm in. Let's do it."

CHAPTER 46

We were dealing with a killer who would expect a turn of events, such as the police tail that had been assigned to me, a tracker being placed in the car I'd been driving, and another one attached on my person as a piece of jewelry so my exact location would be known at all times. The idea was as it always was in cases like this—the killer would take me at a time he assumed was clever enough for him not to be seen or caught by anyone else.

It was a good plan.

It was also a predictable one.

My preference would have been not to go along with it, but in many ways, I felt I had no choice.

I was sitting in James' guesthouse bedroom engaged in a debate over the phone with Cade—one I was not winning. And given I'd just had a similar debate with James, I wasn't up for it.

"I had no idea your case had taken a turn like this," Cade said. "I don't like it. I want you to come home."

"I can't," I said. "Not yet."

"How do they expect you to defend yourself if this guy catches you off-guard? One stab to the chest, Sloane, is all it will take."

"I know. I'm being careful."

Cade sighed. "Please, don't keep pursuing this one. You've done enough already. Let them figure the rest out themselves. Come home to me."

I wanted to go home to him. Even though we'd been together for many years, it had been harder than I expected to be apart so soon after the honeymoon. We were just gearing up for phase two of our lives.

"I need to see this through," I said. "I'm sorry. I know it's not what you want to hear. It will all be over soon."

"You can't know that."

"It's just a feeling I have."

"I'm not going to tell you what to do. You wouldn't listen even if I tried. But can you do something for me? Can you sleep on it tonight? Really think about the risk you're taking over there. It's not the same as the cases you have at home."

Aside from not being able to carry a weapon that fired, it *was* the same. It was no less danger than I always found myself in. The difference was that Australia was foreign to Cade. He'd never been and had formed an opinion in his mind based on what little he did know. He also felt it was different because he wasn't there to protect me.

"I'll think about it," I said. "I'll sleep on it."

I heard a knock at my front door. I walked up and looked out. It was Grace.

"Cade, Grace has come to say goodnight. I'll call you in the morning, okay? I love you."

CHAPTER 47

"Come on in," I said.

Grace nodded and walked inside, sinking down on the couch in the front room. Her conversation with Miller at the police station earlier had been every uncle's worst nightmare. Grace had said little in the way of answering questions, but what she had said over and over again was that Tommy didn't kill Hugh—she did. Unsure what to believe, the police allowed her to return home with James for the night, while they sorted out whom to believe, something I was questioning myself. She'd be questioned again in the morning, and if her answer didn't change, there was a chance she could be arrested.

"How are you doing?" I asked.

She glanced up at me, and the tears started flowing. I reached for a box of tissues and handed it to her. She blew her nose a few times and set the box in her lap.

"It's not fair," she said. "I told them, and they still won't let him go."

"The problem is, you told them the same thing Tommy did, and now they don't know who to believe. One of you isn't telling the truth, and what I don't want to see happen is for you both to be in trouble for it."

"What do you mean?"

"If the police can't be sure which one of you is telling the truth, you could both be held responsible. Did they explain that to you?"

"They said a lot of things. I wasn't listening."

"Murder isn't the only charge a person can go to prison for," I said. "There are other charges you could be convicted for, like murder by association."

"What's that?"

"It's when you help someone else commit murder in some way. Even if you didn't do it yourself, you could spend your entire life in prison for it."

"We could both go to prison, even if only one of us did it?"

"Yes, because you're both confessing to the crime. The police might decide you killed him together, and you'll both go to trial."

"But I didn't know Hugh would fall down the stairs. I was just so angry."

"I know, and I understand how the two of you found yourself in a situation where a hard decision needed to be made. Your uncle understands too. That's why he's been trying to protect you. But he can't do that if you're only concerned about protecting someone else."

She was crying harder now.

"I don't want Tommy to go to jail or prison or anywhere else! It's not fair!"

"You don't deserve to go to prison, either, but if the real truth doesn't come out, both of you could be punished for Hugh's death. I'm sorry to be telling you this, but you need to know."

CHAPTER 48

I woke up the next morning to a photo I'd received from Cade of him sitting on a plane. There was no need to reply. I knew what it meant. I glanced at the time he'd sent it, which was about five hours ago. Depending on layover times, he could arrive in Australia as soon as tonight, and that would change everything.

Aside from the photo, I'd also had a missed call about an hour earlier from an Australian number. I called it back.

"This is Dean," the man said.

"This is Sloane," I said. "I called you yesterday about Caroline."

The phone connection wasn't great. There were cracks in the line, making it hard to hear him.

"I've been off the grid, traveling through a national park in my camper van for the last month. I had no idea she'd died until I went to town last night, turned my phone on like I do when I come into service, and got your call. I'm heading back to the city today and will be talking with the police. I only wished I could have done it sooner."

"I've been trying to locate the man responsible for her murder."

"I can't say for sure, but I have my suspicions."

"I believe her death is related to a project she was working on, a weekend retreat with a group of people who were in hypnotic regression therapy with her."

"I fear you may be right. It was a risky group test to begin with, but Caroline was determined to make a name for herself, and she was sure she was onto something that would change the way we treat specific patients in the future. She'd even started writing her own book based on the research she'd performed."

"What was she doing with the patients she treated during those weekends?"

"It was similar to the treatment already being used, except Caroline believed bringing patients with similar traumatic experiences together would prove to be a more supportive way for them to cope after recovering the lost memories they had been repressing."

"What did you think about what she was doing?"

"I was skeptical."

"Why?"

"When you put a group of people together who have deeply buried trauma, you're rolling the dice on how they'll handle it once it comes out. To tell a therapist is one thing—to tell an entire group is another. I was concerned some might feel vulnerable and ashamed, especially if those in the group didn't respond well to what they heard."

"What was Caroline hoping to achieve by these sessions?"

"Her goal was to prove a support system was a positive method of therapy for patients suffering from blocked memories. She believed those in the group would come together for each other, and the overwhelming support would assist them in healing faster."

"Sounds honorable enough, but you're right—it was risky."

"I wasn't against her finding new avenues to explore. It was the way she went about it that I disliked."

"Meaning?" I asked.

"Each session focused on a single patient while the others offered support and empathy. The patient was given tea before they began, which contained a drug taken from the ayahuasca vine. It's a natural plant found in the Amazon. But natural doesn't mean safe, and while it's grown in Australia and isn't illegal, the extracts taken from acacia plants and mixed with the vine are."

"Did you tell Caroline how you felt about her using it?"

"A few times. I wanted her to cut that part out of her experiment. She didn't listen."

"What does the drug do?" I asked.

"It alters a person's state of consciousness. For some, it has only a little effect. For others, it's far more severe. The user hallucinates, which can last up to six hours. The main problem I had with it is there's no way to predict how a person will respond to it. In my opinion, she could have tested her research without the use of it."

"You gave her your opinions, but you didn't do anything to stop her."

There was a long pause.

"No, I didn't," he said. "I regret it now, just as she regretted the tragic death of one of her patients."

"Do you know what happened to Evan Hall in his session?"

"I don't have all the details. Caroline was so distraught over how it went, she wouldn't really talk about it."

"Was his session the first one she did?"

"It was the second. A woman was the first, and from what Caroline told me, it went very well."

"I believe the other man in the group ended Caroline's life. He blamed her for Evan's death."

There was another pause.

"Mr. Palmer," I said, "are you still there?"

"Yes, I'm still here. Caroline did mention something about him, the patient she didn't get to. She said he was far worse off than the other two."

"In what way?"

"Normally, we wouldn't break the patient's trust by talking about their sessions. We only did it because of my expertise in the area she was researching."

"And what did she say about him?"

"She told me he could be delusional at times, blending past with present, reality with fiction. Other times, he was highly functional and intelligent. Because of this, I warned her to exclude him from the first test group and to use individuals who would accept the treatment more easily, but Caroline felt confident she could help him."

"Do you know anything more about him? Did she ever give you his name, or say anything that would help me locate him?"

"She said his name once. It was an accident. She was talking too fast, and it just slipped out. It's John."

John.

A common name that could take a lifetime for me to figure out the rest, and I still wouldn't have it. They'd used fake names, according to Evan's mother.

"I was told the patient's real names weren't used during their sessions."

"That's right, but I helped her select the candidates for the first round, and as far as I know, the names I was given were their actual given names."

"You don't remember John's surname?" I asked.

"It sounded familiar like something I'd heard before: Falston or Falster, maybe."

It only took a second for my brain to kick in. "Could it have been Falstaff?"

"Yeah, you know something? I think that's right."

CHAPTER 49

The answer to the killer's identity had been in front of me all along, wrapped in pretty packaging, teased and paraded before the police and the local paper, and yet we'd all been oblivious to it. Even I was at fault. But now I had something no one else did yet—clarity.

I ended the call and rushed out the door, running straight into James.

"I was just on my way to see you," he said.

"And I was on my way to see you," I said.

He threw his arms around me, gripping me tightly, a gesture I didn't fully understand. I broke from the embrace and stepped back.

"I'm sorry," he said. "I just wanted to thank you."

"For what?"

"Talking to Grace. This morning she came to me, and we went over everything one more time from start to finish, without anything left out this time. She asked if Tommy pushed Hugh because he was trying to protect her, how could he be saved from going to the bad place."

"So she admitted it wasn't her after all?"

"She will if we can help keep him from going to prison."

"Do you think the story she told you this morning is accurate?"

"It's as accurate as we're going to get. She's still confused about what happened. Tommy is too. But we'll do our best to help them both through it no matter what happens."

"I hope it works out for the best for both of them," I said. "I need to tell you something."

"What's that?"

"I have a name. John Falstaff."

"Are you saying …"

I nodded. "Yes, I am. I believe he's our killer."

CHAPTER 50

There was one John Falstaff living a short drive from the city. As the police focused their efforts on heading to the house to confirm if he was the man, I took another approach. I believed they'd confirm they had their killer, but I also believed he wouldn't be at home when they arrived. He would have anticipated they were getting closer to discovering his identity, and today he'd go out of his way to make sure he remained a step ahead of the rest, just like he always had.

James walked me to the car. "I was hoping you'd hang around here this morning until we get back from the police station."

"You know I can't do that. I have my orders."

"I know what Miller wants. I still wish you would wait a bit longer, though."

I placed a hand on his shoulder. "Everything will be okay. I won't be alone. I have the unmarked police car behind me, and two officers assigned to watch my back. GPS devices, blah, blah, blah. I'm covered."

He sighed because he knew he had no choice other than to relent.

"I still don't have to like it," he said. "Let me know when you get there, all right?"

I slipped inside the car and started the ignition. "You go take care of Grace, and I'll see you all later."

He nodded. "I'm holding you to that."

CHAPTER 51

Ever since I could remember, men had always tried to protect me—from my father, from an abusive boyfriend, from myself. And while their hearts were always in the right place and I'd admired all of them for it, what they failed to realize was that sometimes I needed to validate myself, stand up for myself, on my own two feet, and figure out for myself what was right. I'd risked my life on several occasions, and I'd continue risking it on several more. I'd been smart and stupid, rational and flat-out reckless. One of my favorite modern-day poets said:

see things for what they are
don't waste time pushing through
smoke only to get to a dirty mirror
you're too clean and shiny
and bright for that

And I supposed when I looked back on my life, it summed me up well.

I found a balding, heavily wrinkled Robert Falstaff weeding the garden in front of his house. He wore a loose, white tank top under a pair of overalls and was an elderly, thin slip of a man, who looked like he lived on nothing but the smallest rations of rice. I introduced myself and said I wondered if I could ask him some questions about his son. He agreed and suggested we talk in the house, and I countered, commenting on what a nice day it was before asking if we could remain outside. I wanted to keep things out in the open, where I had more control of the situation.

We walked to a table on his front deck and sat down.

"Was your son named after a character in Shakespeare's plays?" I asked.

"He wasn't. I didn't even know there was a character with his name until John was about seventeen years old and played a small role in the high school's version of *Hamlet*. One of the other kids in the play asked John if he knew his name was the same as the guy in *The Merry Wives of Windsor*, and John said yes. From then on, he told everyone he was named after the man."

"Can I see a photo of John?" I asked.

He shrugged. "I suppose."

He went into the house, returning with an old, tattered photo album. I flipped through it, seeing a boy who appeared shy and frail, but moderately happy, until we reached the pictures of him in his preteen years. His expression had changed. The innocence was gone and had been replaced with an empty, withdrawn look. The photos were still too young for me to make a positive ID, but the features were similar to the man I'd spoken to on the road.

"Do you have any photos of John that are more recent?" I asked.

"Well, I might have, but I'd have to do some digging around. My boy was never big on pictures, especially as he got older. You still haven't told me why you've come here asking about him."

"Were you aware your son was in therapy with a woman who

died recently?" I asked. "Caroline Ashby?"

"I'd heard she died, but he didn't tell me he was in therapy again."

"Again? Was he in therapy when he was younger?"

"He hasn't gone for years now, but he saw someone when he was a kid, and again for a short period of time in his twenties."

"Why was he seeing a therapist?" I asked.

"The first time it was because his mum died. He was depressed. He wouldn't eat, and he often woke up in the middle of the night screaming for her."

"What happened to his mother?"

"Helen? Well, she ... umm ... she killed herself. Overdosed on prescription pills and passed out in the pool. Hard to know whether she drowned herself or whether she just passed out. Either way, she died, and he found her."

"That must have been horrible for him."

"Yeah, he blamed himself."

"But he was just a kid. How was it his fault?"

"There were other circumstances involved. My brother Frank had just died, and Helen and Frank were close. Helen didn't take Frank's death well."

There was a fair amount of confusion in what he'd just said, and I felt like there was a huge gap in the story that he was purposefully leaving out. I decided I'd circle back to it later.

"The second time he went to therapy, what did he go for?" I asked.

"After Helen died, John never fully recovered. He lived in a fantasy world at times, I guess you could say. He was a smart kid, had the highest aptitude test in high school. He could have gone anywhere and had any career."

"What did he end up doing?"

"He was in medical school for a while. He was fascinated with the human body. He enjoyed watching doctors perform surgeries. I thought he'd become one himself."

Bingo. We had ourselves a knife-wielding winner.

"Why didn't he finish med school?"

"When he dropped out, I asked him why, and all he said was he wasn't interested enough in saving people's lives to pursue it."

He wasn't interested in *saving* them, because he was far more interested in *taking* them.

"What does your son do as a career now?" I asked.

"He makes sauces and dips."

"Does he have a business here in town?"

He shook his head. "He sells most of his stuff directly to some of the local markets. A few of the grocery stores carry some of his stuff too. He doesn't need a storefront. The locals just love his food blog."

"His food blog?"

"He posts recipes on there a few times a week along with links on how to purchase the sauces and dips he makes."

"Do you know if there's a photo of your son on his blog?"

He shrugged. "I'm not sure. I'm not on there all that much. I get all the stuff for free, you see, being his father and all."

"Do you know the name of the blogging site or what he calls his business?"

"The Secret's in the Sauce."

I took out my phone and googled the name. The site popped up at the top of the page, and I clicked on it. It was visually beautiful and clean, just like I expected it would be. I scanned the top of the page for the About Me link and clicked on it. At the top was a black-and-white photo of a man, side profile. His face was shaded from the camera. It wasn't much, but it was enough.

I stood up and looked at Robert. "Can you excuse me for a moment? I need to make a phone call."

CHAPTER 52

The secret was no longer just in the sauce. The secret was out. And although the photo of John Falstaff wasn't front-facing and was shadowed, one item he was wearing really clinched it for me. He wore a fedora—the same, exact fedora I'd seen him in.

I called Miller, confirming the man whose name I'd given this morning was the same man whom I'd spoken to along the road. He was grateful for the tip and responded in kind, telling me they were sifting through things at John Falstaff's house, which Tommy had confirmed was the place he'd been taken. John wasn't there, and it seemed he had no plan to return. He had left a note on the table stating as much. Concerned he had a runner, Miller sent officers to the airport, anticipating John was about to leave the country and go off the grid.

I agreed John was going off the grid, but I felt he'd stick much closer to home, finding a way to blend in, possibly even reinventing himself. Cairns had a well-known, friendly backpacker community and was a place every type of person visited from a myriad of countries. All John had to do was make a few changes to his look, and he'd fit right in.

When I walked back to the table, Robert was sitting there, patiently waiting.

"What is it you think my son has done?" he asked.

"It may be hard for you to take."

He shrugged. "My life has been hard to take, but here I am, still living. Go on now and just say it."

For all the times in the past when I couldn't put the brakes on my nonstop blathering, I found myself wanting to spare him the details of what his son had so violently done.

"I believe he murdered Caroline Ashby and Adelaide Wiggins," I said. "And he tried to murder Senator Ashby."

"How do you know? What evidence do you have to prove it?"

The way he said it gave me the impression he was curious, but not startled by what I'd said.

"I met your son," I said. "I didn't know his name at the time, but he confessed what he'd done to me."

"And you're sure you have the right man?"

I nodded.

Robert drummed his fingers along the table, thinking. "I see."

I crossed my arms. "You don't seem shocked to hear about what your son has done."

"I've always known what he was capable of, I suppose."

"What do you mean?" I asked.

"My son can be ruthless at times, that's all."

Only it wasn't all. Just looking at him, I could tell. He knew things, dark things I imagined he didn't want to talk about, and I wondered if he'd known of his son's character flaw because there had been a time when he'd struggled with the same one himself. Sitting in front of me now with heavy bags under his eyes and a crooked back, it seemed time had made him a different man than I imagined he once was.

"My son is not a bad person," he said. "He really isn't. He's just been troubled from time to time. I blame myself for it."

"How is it your fault?"

"I didn't know how to deal with his pain and suffering after Helen died, and I wasn't around a lot. Looking back now, I can see he didn't have the support he needed. It was a different time then. People didn't talk through things like they do now. We just shoved it down so far inside ourselves, it never had the chance to come up again."

"I'm sorry to be the one to have to tell you what's happened. The police are at John's place now, going through his things. He knew they were coming and left a note saying he wouldn't return. Any idea where he might go?"

His father bowed his head and remained silent for a time. I waited. The conversation hadn't been easy. Not for me, and not for him. The least I could do was to offer whatever patience I could. After a minute, he pushed his chair back and stood.

"I'm tired," he said. "I need rest."

"I understand. Would you be willing to answer my question before I leave?"

"I just can't talk about this anymore," he said. "I know it's not what you want to hear, but I just …"

As his words trailed off, his eyes began to roll back into his head. He tried to take a step forward and stumbled, crashing down on the deck below. I dropped to my knees next to him.

"Mr. Falstaff? Are you all right?"

He didn't respond.

I ran out of the yard, waving my arms in the air at the police sitting in wait nearby. "Something's wrong with John's father. Call for an ambulance."

CHAPTER 53

Robert Falstaff had suffered a stroke, but it was minor, and he would recover. He'd been picked up and transported to the hospital for testing. I walked to my car and got inside, feeling a tremendous amount of guilt over the role I felt I'd played in what had just happened to him. I thought about all I'd said, wishing I would have listened to my inner voice and held off on telling him his son was a barbaric killer. But not telling him wouldn't have done him any favors. He would have found out either way.

Miller had hoped that sending me to visit Robert would allow John the perfect opportunity to corner me, and when he did, the officers keeping an eye on me would be ready to take him out. But unless John had been hiding, he hadn't shown. I wondered where he was and what he was planning next. Cade would be here soon. I was running out of time.

I returned to James' house, and no one was there. I figured they were all still at the police station, ironing out Grace's story. It was hard to know which story offered the truth in its entirety or whether none of them did, but I believed what happened that night came down to two scared kids who thought they were doing what had to be done. I hoped the police would see it that way too.

My phone rang. It was James.

"I just received a security alert on the guesthouse," he said. "Where are you?"

"I just got back to your place. What kind of an alert?"

"It happens when the alarm goes off and isn't reset. I was hoping you'd forgotten to reset it after you went inside."

"I just got out of the car. I haven't made it to the guesthouse yet."

"Where are the police officers assigned to you?"

"They just parked," I said. "They're heading over to me now to check on the house before I go in."

"Good. Let me know if they find anything."

I ended the call and spoke to the officers about the possible security breach. They readied their weapons and opened the door to the guesthouse, telling me to wait outside until they returned. For the next few minutes, all was quiet, and then the officers emerged, this time with their weapons holstered.

"I don't know what to say," one officer said. "It's all clear. Must have been a false alarm."

"All right," I said. "Thanks for checking."

"We're going to secure the main house, and then we'll be in the car if you need anything."

I nodded, and they walked away.

Even though I'd been given the green light, I hesitated. James' security system had never been faulty before. I had a hard time believing whatever happened had been a random glitch.

I sent James a text, letting him know it had been secured and reset, and I asked when they expected to return. He responded that they were headed back now.

I walked into the house, tossed my keys into the bowl on the counter, and heard a shattering sound toward the back of the house that sounded like breaking glass. The house alarm triggered again. I ran through the house toward the sound, tripping over something small and hard when I reached the living room. I crashed to the ground, my head smacking against the wood floor. I glanced up, staring at the baseball I'd just tumbled over. My forehead felt hot and sticky. I wiped my hand across it and held it in front of me, staring at my palm. It was bloody, and I wasn't alone. *He* was here with me. But where?

I scrambled to my feet, my head swirling as I headed back to the door. Halfway there, a hand grabbed me from behind, yanking me into the bedroom as I passed it. I was hurled onto the bed. The bedroom door smacked shut, and as I struggled to stand, the knife he was holding tore into me, slicing a five-inch gash down the side of my chest.

I reeled back against the wall. Blood spilled down my abdomen. I needed to stop it, but I couldn't. There wasn't time.

John charged at me a second time, the knife slashing through the air. I raised my leg, cracking it into his kneecap before he got the opportunity to cut me again. The blow was enough to send him flying backward, but not enough to stop him. He charged me again, shouting, "This doesn't have to be painful. Stop moving, and this will all be over."

"Go to hell!" I screamed.

I yanked the side-table drawer open, pulling out the trusted homemade remedy I'd made a few days earlier, and as he swung at me again, I showered his face with pepper spray.

I could hear the two officers running down the hall in our direction.

"Sloane! You in here?" one of them said.

"I'm in the bedroom."

They reached the door. It was locked. I ran toward it, and John reached for my leg, stopping me. I kicked back, trying to break free, but the grip he had on me was too tight.

"Come through that door and she dies!" John yelled.

"Don't listen to him!" I answered.

I slammed my foot down on his hand, and he yelped in pain. He reached down, wrapping his arm around my neck and whispered, "To thine own self be true. Isn't that right, Sloane Monroe?" and as the dagger slashed toward my chest, I drove my knee into his groin. I tried to stand but fell back onto the bed. I was weak and had lost too much blood.

Outside of the bedroom window, a large figure loomed. Noel raised his gun, gave me a slight nod, and then fired. The bullet tore through the window, piercing the side of John's neck. He flopped backward onto the ground, dropped the knife, and wrapped both hands around his wound as if he believed he could save himself. But it was far too late for that.

As the two officers broke down the door, I crawled over to John and grabbed his chin, looking him in the eye as he drew his final breath. I said, "Thou art unfit for any place but hell."

CHAPTER 54

I opened my eyes to the familiar surroundings of the hospital, only this time Cade was hovering over me.

"I'm glad you're here," I said.

He wrapped my hands inside his. "I'm glad you're alive."

"It's over now. He's dead."

"I heard. Looks like you'll have a few scars from your ordeal earlier today."

I smiled. "I'll just add them to my growing collection."

There was a knock on the hospital room door. We looked over. Robert Falstaff peeked in and said, "Hi there, can I come in?"

I nodded.

"I've just spoken with the police," he said. "They filled me in on what happened to you. I'm glad you're all right."

"I'm sorry I was so forward when I saw you yesterday," I said. "If I would have known what would happen, I would not have been so bold."

"It's all good. I'm feeling much better now."

"I'm also sorry about your son. No matter what John did, he was still your child."

I glanced at Cade, who had just put together whom I was talking to. He moved closer to me, standing so close he was like a human shield.

I squeezed his hand. "Cade, it's okay."

Cade stared at Robert. "I know it is," which was his way of letting us both know he wasn't budging.

"I wondered if I could talk to you for a minute," Robert said.

"Sure," I said. "What's on your mind?"

"I wanted to tell you something I should have before. It's something I should have dealt with a long time ago and didn't. Maybe if I had, my son wouldn't have turned out the way he did. Maybe he would have had a chance."

"Okay."

"When he was young, his mum had been stepping out on me, you see, with my brother. At some point, John must have found out about it, but he never said anything to me. I'm not sure why. Maybe he was trying to spare my feelings. What I do know is that my wife had planned on leaving us and running off with my brother. John must have overheard them talking about it, and it upset him."

At such a young age, he was about to be abandoned by a person who was supposed to love him. I couldn't imagine what he must have felt.

"One morning, my brother and I went for a hike," Robert said. "We took John. At a point during the hike, my brother got his camera out to take a photo. He got too close to the edge and slipped over the side. I ran to help him, but John got there first. He leaned toward my brother and told him he hated him and that he wouldn't let him ruin his life or his family. Then John did something I didn't expect—he kicked his uncle in the face. My brother lost what little grip he had, and I stood there, watching my brother fall to his death, knowing my son had killed him."

"What did you do?" I asked.

"I knew then something was off about John, but I think I'd always known. I just hadn't wanted to accept it. I could have told the police what really happened, but I didn't. I said my brother fell over the side, and that was the end of it. When my wife found out what happened, she killed herself. John was devastated. I thought eventually he'd be okay, but he was never okay after that. Some people might say his actions aren't my fault, but in a way, they have always been. And I just thought it was time to tell the truth. Probably sounds crazy, but it's what he would have wanted."

"Did you ever talk to John about what happened?"

"I didn't. It's one of my biggest regrets. Anyway, I just wanted you to know."

He nodded and walked out of the room.

"Do you think if he would have told the police what really happened back then, John would have turned out differently?" Cade asked.

I shrugged. "It's hard to say."

Noel, James, Victoria, and Grace entered the room. Grace was carrying a giant stuffed koala in her hands that had balloons attached to it. She ran to the bed and threw her arms around me.

"I picked the koala out myself," she said. "I hope you like it."

"I love it," I said.

James held a hand out to Cade, and they shook.

"You must be the husband," he said. "It's good to meet you."

"You too," Cade said.

"How are you feeling?" Victoria asked.

"A bit beaten up, but otherwise all right."

While the men talked, she bent down and whispered, "I talked to James."

I smiled. "And?"

"The feeling's mutual."

"I'm glad."

Noel walked over and patted me on the head. "Glad you're going to be okay."

"Thanks," I said, "for saving my life."

He winked. "Oh, I don't know about that. The man was far worse off than you were when I saw him. I just made sure he stayed that way."

James looked at Cade and said, "We'd love for you two to stay longer. I'd be happy to be your tour guide for a few days."

Cade looked at me. "What do you think?"

I sat up, pondering the idea. "I'd like to take you up on that sometime, but for now, it's time for me to go home."

ABOUT CHERYL BRADSHAW

Cheryl Bradshaw is a *New York Times* and *USA Today* bestselling author writing in the genres of mystery, thriller, paranormal suspense, and romantic suspense. Her novel *Stranger in Town* (Sloane Monroe series #4) was a 2013 Shamus Award finalist for Best PI Novel of the Year, and her novel *I Have a Secret* (Sloane Monroe series #3) was a 2013 eFestival of Words winner for Best Thriller. Since 2013, seven of Cheryl's novels have made the *USA Today* bestselling books list.

Books by Cheryl Bradshaw

Sloane Monroe Series

Black Diamond Death (Book 1)
Charlotte Halliwell has a secret. But before revealing it to her sister, she's found dead.

Murder in Mind (Book 2)
A woman is found murdered, the serial killer's trademark "S" carved into her wrist.

I Have a Secret (Book 3)
Doug Ward has been running from his past for twenty years. But after his fourth whisky of the night, he doesn't want to keep quiet, not anymore.

Stranger in Town (Book 4)
A frantic mother runs down the aisles, searching for her missing daughter. But little Olivia is already gone.

Bed of Bones (Book 5)
Sometimes even the deepest, darkest secrets find their way to the surface.

Flirting with Danger (Book 5.5) A Sloane Monroe Short Story
A fancy hotel. A weekend getaway. For Sloane Monroe, rest has finally arrived, until the lights go out, a woman screams, and Sloane's nightmare begins.

Hush Now Baby (Book 6)
Serena Westwood tiptoes to her baby's crib and looks inside, startled to find her newborn son is gone.

Dead of Night (Book 6.5) A Sloane Monroe Short Story
After her mother-in-law is fatally stabbed, Wren is seen fleeing with the bloody knife. Is Wren the killer, or is a dark, scandalous family secret to blame?

Gone Daddy Gone (Book 7)
A man lurks behind Shelby in the park. Who is he? And why does he have a gun?

Sloane Monroe Stories: Deadly Sins

Deadly Sins: Sloth (Book 1)
Darryl has been shot, and a mysterious woman is sprawled out on the floor in his hallway. She's dead too. Who is she? And why have they both been murdered?

Deadly Sins: Wrath (Book 2)
Headlights flash through Maddie's car's back windshield, someone following close behind. When her car careens into a nearby tree, the chase comes to an end. But for Maddie, the end is just the beginning.

Deadly Sins: Lust (Book 3)
Marissa Calhoun sits alone on a beach-like swimming hole nestled on Australia's foreshore. Tonight the lagoon is hers and hers alone. Or is it?

Addison Lockhart Series

Grayson Manor Haunting (Book 1)
When Addison Lockhart inherits Grayson Manor after her mother's untimely death, she unlocks a secret that's been kept hidden for over fifty years.

Rosecliff Manor Haunting (Book 2)
Addison Lockhart jolts awake. The dream had seemed so real. Eleven-year-old twins Vivian and Grace were so full of life, but they couldn't be. They've been dead for over forty years.

Blackthorn Manor Haunting (Book 3)
Addison Lockhart leans over the manor's window, gasping when she feels a hand on her back. She grabs the windowsill to brace herself, but it's too late--she's already falling.

Till Death do us Part Novella Series

Whispers of Murder (Book 1)
It was Isabelle Donnelly's wedding day, a moment in time that should have been the happiest in her life...until it ended in murder.

Echoes of Murder (Book 2)
When two women are found dead at the same wedding, medical examiner Reagan Davenport will stop at nothing to discover the identity of the killer.

Stand-Alone Novels

Eye for Revenge
Quinn Montgomery wakes to find herself in the hospital. Her childhood best friend Evie is dead, and Evie's four-year-old son witnessed it all. Traumatized over what he saw, he hasn't spoken.

The Perfect Lie
When true-crime writer Alexandria Weston is found murdered on the last stop of her book tour, fellow writer Joss Jax steps in to investigate.

Hickory Dickory Dead
Maisie Fezziwig wakes to a harrowing scream outside. Curious, she walks outside to investigate, and Maisie stumbles on a grisly murder that will change her life forever.

Roadkill
Suburban housewife Juliette Granger has been living a secret life ... a life that's about to turn deadly for everyone she loves.

Non-Fiction

Arise
Arise is a collection of motivational stories written by women who have been where you may find yourself today. Their stories are raw, real, heartfelt, and inspiring.

Made in the USA
Middletown, DE
17 June 2024